W9-BVK-855

the
jerk
magnet

Books by Melody Carlson

Life at Kingston High

the jerk
magnet

Melody Carlson

Revell

a division of Baker Publishing Group
Grand Rapids, Michigan

© 2012 by Melody Carlson

Published by Revell
a division of Baker Publishing Group
P.O. Box 6287, Grand Rapids, MI 49516-6287
www.revellbooks.com

Printed in the United States of America

All rights reserved. No part of this publication may be reproduced, stored in a retrieval system, or transmitted in any form or by any means—for example, electronic, photocopy, recording—without the prior written permission of the publisher. The only exception is brief quotations in printed reviews.

Library of Congress Cataloging-in-Publication Data
Carlson, Melody.
    The jerk magnet / Melody Carlson.
        p.   cm. — (Life at Kingston High ; bk. 1)
    Summary: When sixteen-year-old Chelsea Martin's future stepmother gives
her a total makeover, she attracts all of the wrong boys and drives away many
girls, but her friend Janelle keeps telling Chelsea to be true to herself, while
helping her find a way to catch the eye of Nicholas, the one "non-jerk" at
school.
        ISBN 978-0-8007-1962-3 (pbk.)
        [1. Beauty, Personal—Fiction. 2. Interpersonal relations—Fiction. 3.
Self-perception—Fiction. 4. High schools—Fiction. 5. Schools—Fiction.
6. Christian life—Fiction. 7. Family life—California—Fiction. 8. Remarriage—
Fiction. 9. California—Fiction.] I. Title.
PZ7.C216637Jdr 2012
[Fic]—dc23   2011028447

This book is a work of fiction. Names, characters, places, and incidents are the product of the author's imagination or are used fictitiously. Any resemblance to actual events, locales, or persons, living or dead, is coincidental.

The internet addresses, email addresses, and phone numbers in this book are accurate at the time of publication. They are provided as a resource. Baker Publishing Group does not endorse them or vouch for their content or permanence.

one

Sometimes the best way to handle rejection is to simply expect it. Just accept that antagonism is coming your way and get beyond it as quickly and quietly as possible. At least that was what Chelsea Martin had been telling herself since hitting adolescence. But with two more years of high school lurking ahead, her resolve, not to mention her patience, had worn thin. And she wondered . . . just how old did her peers have to become before they eventually grew up? Forty-eight, perhaps? Maybe by their thirtieth class reunion they would treat people humanely and with an iota of respect.

Consequently, no one at her school was happier to see June arrive and the school year end than Chelsea. With almost three blessed months before she'd be forced to reenter that adolescent torture chamber, she planned to spend the summer underground, geeking out on her phony Facebook page, reading sci-fi and fantasy, and catching up on her favorite reality shows. Not exactly high aspirations, but after an academically packed year as well as keeping her GPA high enough to remain in the top ten of her class, she concurred with the old McDonald's slogan—she *did* deserve a break today. But then, after just one week of sleeping in and vegging out, her "vacation" was cut short.

The madness began on Saturday morning. Awakened from a deep sleep and a delicious dream (Rob Pattinson was vying for her affection), Chelsea was in no mood to "rise and shine!" But there was Dad, standing over her wearing a silly apron that said "Kiss the Cook" and a grin that spelled nothing but trouble. Plus he had a pancake turner in his hand.

"Go away," she said, longing to escape back into her dream. Although it was probably too late since Rob (aka Edward Cullen) had already vanished into the misty twilit forest.

"Up and at 'em," Dad hailed in a painfully cheery tone.

"Is the house on fire or what?" Chelsea demanded.

"No, I just want you to get up. Come on, Chels. I'm fixing your favorite—blueberry pancakes!"

"I don't want any pancakes." She groaned and rolled over. It wasn't even nine o'clock. And since when were blueberry pancakes her favorite? Did he think she was still seven? All she wanted at the moment was to return to her dream and that dreamy Edward.

"Come on, Chels." Dad changed his tone from cheerful to pitiful. "We haven't really talked all week. I miss you, sweetie."

She sat up and sighed. That was actually true—they hadn't talked much lately, maybe not even for two weeks. But that was Dad's fault, not hers. All Dad did was work, work, work.

"Come on," he urged her. "I already heated the griddle. And the coffee's brewing and—"

6

"Okay, okay." She reluctantly crawled out of bed, shoved her feet into her pink bunny slippers, and shuffled her way toward the kitchen. Sure enough, Dad really was making pancakes, complete with fresh blueberries.

"What's the special occasion?" she asked as she filled a mug with coffee and sat down at the breakfast bar, gazing blurrily at him.

"Just us." He grinned broadly, and she was surprised to see his dimples make an appearance. She'd almost forgotten he had them. The dimples combined with his messy bed-head hair, plaid flannel pajama pants, and faded blue T-shirt were surprisingly endearing—almost enough to wipe out her suspicions that something was seriously wrong. But not quite.

"Uh-huh . . . just us. Right." She tried to suppress her skepticism as she spooned sugar into her coffee.

"You know, father and daughter hanging out and eating blueberry pancakes together." Another spoonful of batter sizzled onto the hot griddle, releasing a delicious crispy smell and almost making her hungry.

She still wasn't awake enough to put her finger on it, but something was definitely not jiving here. Why was Dad acting so weird? Did he think he was running for Father of the Year, or something worse? She glanced around the kitchen, wondering if there might be a hidden camera somewhere. Maybe he was auditioning for a father-daughter reality show.

"Okay," she said carefully, "what's *really* up with you, Dad?"

Both his boyish grin and his dimples faded. "We need to talk."

She took in a quick breath. "If I was your girlfriend, those four little words would have me seriously freaking." She was trying to be funny, but the truth was she did feel worried.

What had she done to warrant a "talk"? She couldn't remember any particular offense. It was pretty hard to break the rules when you didn't even have a life to start with.

She dipped her spoon in the sugar bowl again. It wasn't that she didn't like coffee, she just liked it sweetened up—a lot.

Dad dumped another circle of batter, using the bottom of the ladle to enlarge it. "Well, as a matter of fact, this *is* about my girlfriend."

"Huh?" Chelsea's hand stopped in midair. With her third spoonful of sugar halfway between the sugar bowl and her coffee mug, she gaped at her dad. She could tell by his creased brow that he was feeling very uncomfortable about something, like he was about to disclose some bad news, something he knew Chelsea would not want to hear. It reminded her of that time more than five years ago when he'd told her the worst news imaginable. But nothing could possibly be that terrible.

"Your girlfriend?" she asked. "What girlfriend would that be?"

"Kate, of course."

"Kate?" Chelsea tried to wrap her head around this. She barely knew Kate. In some ways she seemed almost like an imaginary person to Chelsea. Like someone she'd seen on a TV show or passed on the street. Kate was beautiful, stylish, perfect . . . and a perfect stranger to Chelsea. Dad was calling this Kate his girlfriend now?

"Yes . . . Kate." He flipped his pancakes, acting preoccupied and focused, like he hadn't just said something totally out of left field. Like he didn't get that Chelsea still considered her mom the only woman in his life. Like he didn't know how creepy it sounded to hear him use the word *girlfriend* when he was referring to himself. What was wrong with the man? Didn't he know that dads don't have girlfriends? Not her dad anyway.

Chelsea had been eleven when her mom suffered an aneurism and died almost instantly. Mom's death had blindsided and devastated Chelsea and her dad. Even five years later, it was still hard for her to think about it. And up until recently, Chelsea's dad had shown absolutely no interest in dating anyone. That was okay with Chelsea. So far the two of them had managed just fine on their own. Housekeeping was a bit random and haphazard, but there'd been no real complaints. Chelsea was used to doing her part.

Then Kate Bradley came along . . . and Dad had cautiously reentered the dating world. He'd reassured Chelsea it was "nothing serious," and she had believed him. In fact, it had been somewhat amusing seeing her dad worried about how to act and what to say on a date. In some ways Chelsea thought the experience was probably good for him. She'd even been a little envious, wishing she had someone to date too—like that would ever happen. But during this relatively short amount of time, Chelsea had never once heard Dad call Kate his girlfriend. That word alone was totally unnerving. Still, she planned to play it cool. Perhaps like other aggravations in life, this too would pass.

"So . . . tell me, Dad, what's up with Kate?" She took a sip of her sweetened coffee, trying to act perfectly normal.

"Well, honey, I've been meaning to tell you that it's been getting more serious."

Chelsea frowned. She didn't even know it was serious, and now it was *more* serious? "You guys only go out once a week at the most. You've probably had a total of six dates and—"

"Oh, it's been a lot more than six dates, Chels. We meet for lunch occasionally, and we go for—"

"But how is a couple months long enough to get *serious*, Dad?" It was bizarre, but for some reason she felt like the parent now. Like she needed to advise him about the dangers of dating and getting serious.

"Sometimes you just know about these things." He neatly flipped a pancake.

"Know what about what things?" She knew her tone was too sharp. She could tell by his expression that she sounded rude and angry. Okay, maybe she was angry.

"You know when it's right . . . when you've met the right one."

"The right *what*?"

"The right, uh . . . soul mate."

She blinked. "Kate is your soul mate?"

He set the pancakes on a plate and handed it to her. "She is, Chelsea." He nodded in an assured way. "I know it."

"But how can you possibly *know* that?"

"Because I just do." He poured new circles of batter onto the hot griddle. "To be honest, I think I've known it almost from the start."

"Are you saying that you've been in love with Kate since you met her?" She glared at him. "And you never even told me about this? You didn't give me any kind of warning whatsoever?"

"I guess I was in denial." He slid the bottle of maple syrup toward her, followed by the butter dish. "I honestly didn't think it would be possible to love someone else again."

"Maybe it's not possible." Even as she said this, she knew she sounded ridiculous. Lots of people fell in and out of love every single day. She saw it at school all the time. Of course, they were just kids and most of them were dumber than dirt anyway. Dad was in his late forties.

"I know it's going to take some time for you to process this." He set an empty plate next to the sizzling pancakes. "I'm sure it's kind of a shock. But I need you to try to understand. Okay?"

With her lips tightly together, she nodded. Spearing a large section of pancake with her fork, she crammed it into her mouth, but the pancake tasted like sawdust, like it was turning into a large, hard lump that would probably stick in her throat. Perhaps it would lodge there and choke her to death. Just the same, she swallowed it. Maybe she didn't care if she choked. So what if she died on her dad's blueberry pancakes. But worried she really couldn't breathe, she took a big gulp of coffee, and even though it washed the glob down, the liquid was so hot it made her eyes water. Now Dad would assume she was crying.

"Anyway, Chelsea . . ." His eyes were on his pancakes, like they needed his full attention. "I proposed to Kate last night. I asked her to marry me."

Chelsea wanted to scream or to throw something. What was wrong with her dad? Why was he doing this? But he was so focused on turning the second string of pancakes that it looked like he was in some kind of cooking competition. Perhaps a blueberry pancake trophy was at stake.

"And Kate said yes." Dad peered at Chelsea like he thought she'd be delighted by this news. Did he expect her to say congratulations?

"Oh." She pushed her plate away. What little appetite she'd had was completely gone. "So . . . you and Kate will be getting married then. Wow, that's just great, Dad." Her words dripped with sarcasm. "I hope the two of you will be very happy together."

He looked hurt. "I know you'll need to get used to this, but I want you to understand that—"

"Yeah, I know. I'll get used to it." She nodded, blinking back real tears. "I'm not hungry, Dad."

"Oh, Chelsea." He turned off the stove and hurried around the island. Before she could escape, he wrapped his arms around her. "The last thing I want to do is hurt you. You're my best buddy, Chels."

She wanted to point out that she *used* to be his best buddy. Obviously he'd found someone else now. But she knew if she tried to speak, she'd start blubbering like a baby. This whole thing was bad enough without adding stupid tears.

"This doesn't change anything between us, Chels. You probably don't feel like that's true right now, but you'll see in time that having Kate as part of our family will make everything better—for both of us."

"Right." Her voice sounded gruff. Pulling away from him, she stepped back. "I just need some space right now."

"You don't want your pancakes?"

"No. Thank. You." She stepped back farther, preparing to dash back to her room, slam the door, and try to make sense of why Dad was doing this to her.

"There's more," he said in an even more serious tone. "Please don't run off yet, Chelsea."

"There's more?" she said. "What do you mean, *more*? Don't tell me that Kate has a bunch of kids and that I'm going to have to share my room and babysit and—"

"No, no, Kate doesn't have any kids."

"Is she *pregnant*?"

"No, of course not." He frowned at Chelsea like she'd just made some sort of nasty insinuation. Maybe she had. Maybe she didn't care.

"Well, what is it then?" She planted her hands on her hips, glaring and waiting.

"My job is getting transferred to San Jose."

"Huh?"

"San Jose, California. We have to move in six weeks, honey."

"We have to *move*?" She shouted this back at him like it was the worst news ever, when in truth she didn't even care that much. Still, he didn't need to know her true feelings. Especially since he seemed to enjoy being generally clueless about her. Why not throw a hissy fit over moving—didn't he deserve some friction?

"I know it's a lot to take in—"

"So let me get this clear." She shook a fist in the air. "Not only are you turning my life totally upside down by getting married to someone you hardly know, someone I've barely even met, but now you're forcing me to move away from the only home I've ever known. You're making me change schools right before my junior year?" She glared at him. "What's next, Dad? Am I going to find out that you plan to sell me into the international slave market and use my college savings to buy you and Kate a new love nest in Bermuda?"

"Chelsea!" He frowned in a disappointed way.

"I'm just saying."

"Look, I don't have a choice in the job change. The company is downsizing, and several other executives are being laid off right now. I'm actually fortunate to still have a job—in a way, it's a promotion."

"Well, that's just peachy, Dad. You're getting married and you're moving me out of my home and halfway across the country. I just couldn't be happier." She turned and ran from the room. And she did slam her door. Juvenile, yes, but necessary all the same.

She flopped onto her bed, wishing she had a good friend to call and vent to, but the truth was her closest friend, Sharee from drama, was just not that good a friend. In fact, Chelsea hadn't had a real best friend since middle school—back when she and Virginia had been inseparable. In fourth grade they went to youth group together, and together they professed to follow Jesus and promised to be best friends forever. As it turned out, both commitments turned out to be short-lived.

Chelsea went over to her dresser and picked up a framed photo. It had been taken on her twelfth birthday, right after Chelsea had gotten braces and zits. Virginia had fared better on her twelfth birthday—she'd gotten a pink cell phone and breasts. Although both girls were smiling in the photo, with their other friends gathered in the background, she could see the truth in Virginia's face. Chelsea had been oblivious on her big night—she'd begged her still grief-stricken dad for that slumber party. She later saw (with twenty-twenty hindsight) what had really been going on at the time.

Virginia had coaxed Chelsea's other so-called friends (other youth group girls) to come that night, for what was probably a true pity party. Feeling sorry for Chelsea because it had been only three months since her mom's death, the girls had shown up to celebrate Chelsea's birthday. Pathetic, considering those girls were finished with Chelsea by then. As soon as seventh grade started, they left her in the dust. Chelsea never went back to church or youth group again.

Even now, it still bewildered Chelsea the way Virginia and her circle of picture-perfect friends had made that amazing transition—it seemed like overnight—abandoning bikes and Barbies for boys and fashion. But Chelsea hadn't been invited to cross that bridge with them. Probably because she was incapable, handicapped, broken—or maybe she'd been too distracted by her own grief. At least that's what she'd consoled herself with back then.

She studied the photo, seeing that kinky, mud-colored hair, those ugly braces—which she got shortly before everyone else got theirs off—and those horrible zits that seemed to have popped out of nowhere and just never went away. Though not everything showed in that photo—like her complete lack of breasts and deep-rooted insecurities—thanks to her many shortcomings, Chelsea became an overnight misfit, and she'd spent the next four years trying to disappear or blend into the walls at school . . . hoping to survive.

And now her dad was not only asking her to start over at a new school—where she'd have to learn all over again how to slip beneath the radar—but he was bringing his own picture-perfect "soul mate" into their previously comfortable little world. Really, could life get any worse?

two

After nearly a week of serious sulking, in which she'd gotten fairly sick of herself, Chelsea decided it was time to be a good sport. Really, it was pointless to protest since, like so many other things in her life, she had no control over the outcome anyway. Why not just go along with it—or at least pretend to. She consoled herself in thinking that someday she would be an adult and she'd move out on her own, and then she would live life according to her own rules.

"I really want you in my wedding," Kate was saying to Chelsea as they ate dinner together. This was Dad's recovery plan for Chelsea—take her to dinner with her stepmother-to-be and see if he couldn't get the two females to bond over a chocolate dessert.

However, they'd been over this I-want-you-in-my-wedding topic several times already tonight, and Chelsea felt certain that she'd made her position completely clear. "Thanks anyway," she told Kate, "but like I said, I'm just not into that sort of thing. I don't like standing up in front of a bunch of people."

"But it's going to be a very small wedding," Kate said.

Chelsea looked at Dad—like, *help!*

He turned to Kate. "You know, I'd love for Chelsea to be in the wedding just as much as you would, sweetie. But only if Chels *wants* to do it." He held up his hands. "And it seems that she doesn't."

Kate's pretty pink lips twisted into a disappointed pout.

"Sorry, Kate." Chelsea lowered her eyes as she took a small sip of water. If only this torturous evening could come to a swift and painless end. Suddenly she felt tempted to slip off to the bathroom . . . where she would pull the fire alarm and act completely surprised as the patrons were evacuated from the restaurant—and she could go home.

Unless Chelsea was imagining things, Kate's pout suddenly transformed itself into a rather catty smile. She pushed a thick strand of silky blonde hair over a tanned shoulder, then pointed a perfectly manicured shell-pink nail at her soon-to-be stepdaughter. "I think I know what's troubling you," she said. She leaned forward, peering intently at Chelsea, studying her closely as if she were taking some kind of inventory. Similar to the way some girls, particularly mean girls, would look at Chelsea at school.

A prickly heat climbed up Chelsea's neck and flushed her cheeks. This was her normal reaction to embarrassing situations. She loathed being the center of attention under any circumstances, but feeling like a biology specimen in a public place, especially a restaurant, was way beyond freaky.

Kate nodded with a knowing expression. "Chelsea, I understand you better than you realize," she continued. "In fact, I know exactly what your problem is."

Well, of course Kate knew what Chelsea's problem was.

Everyone at Chelsea's school knew what her problem was. Even the guy waiting their table knew what her problem was. She was just plain unattractive, bordering on ugly. To make matters worse, she was painfully shy, along with a bunch of other unfortunate things she'd rather not think about. Seriously, did they really have to discuss this right here and now?

Chelsea shot her dad another pleading look, but he wasn't looking at her. No, his eyes were locked onto his gorgeous fiancée's face, staring at Kate as if totally mesmerized by her loveliness. The phrase "the sun and the moon rises and sets on her" passed through Chelsea's head. It was obvious Dad was in deep.

"You simply lack confidence, Chelsea," Kate stated with absolute certainty.

Chelsea stopped herself from saying "duh" and rolling her eyes.

"And I know exactly what you need to get you past this." Kate gave Chelsea a smug little smile, like she thought she'd just discovered plutonium or the cure for colon cancer.

It took all of Chelsea's self-control not to bolt out of the restaurant, or go for the fire alarm. Instead, she took a deep breath and silently counted to ten. Sometimes that worked.

Kate pointed at Chelsea again. Didn't she know it was rude to point? "You and I are going shopping tomorrow." Kate turned to Dad. "That's okay with you, isn't it?"

He shrugged. "If Chelsea wants to."

"Because I know how to help her," Kate told Dad. "If Chelsea will let me, I can help her to change her life."

Dad's brows drew together. "By shopping?"

Kate laughed. "Well, that and some other things. But

she has to trust me *implicitly*." She pointed at Dad. "And so do you."

He leaned forward, looking intently into Kate's big blue eyes. "You know I trust you, Kate." He touched the solitaire ring on her left hand. "How much more could I trust anyone?"

"Good." Kate patted his cheek. "And that's why we'll be using your employee discount to do some serious shopping tomorrow."

He looked interested. "You're going to shop at our store?"

"Why not go where 'designers' best costs you less'?" She quoted one of the lame advertisement lines of the discount clothing chain that Dad worked for. "How do you beat Best 4 Less?" she chirped. "Combine their already low prices along with your discount—and we're talking bargains with a capital B."

Chelsea couldn't help but groan. Dad tossed her a warning look. But Kate continued in oblivion. "I couldn't help but notice the new shipment in the back room when I met you for lunch on Thursday. It should all be on the floor by now. In fact, I'd like to do some shopping myself—with an employee discount." She winked at Chelsea like they were sharing some special sort of secret.

Chelsea knew that Kate had managed one of the discount outlet stores until she and Dad began dating, and due to the company's no-dating policy, Kate had been forced to find a different job. Of course, Chelsea had learned of this—and so much more—only recently.

"We are going to give you a total makeover this summer," Kate told Chelsea. "And then we'll start working on your confidence and self-esteem, which is the real key to beauty."

Chelsea shot Dad another look, but she realized she was on her own in this. Clearly in over his head, Dad was too smitten to be of any help.

"Trust me, Chelsea," Kate assured her, "by the time you start school in San Jose, you will be a completely new woman."

Chelsea experienced a schizophrenic conglomeration of emotions—primarily an enormous pile of extreme humiliation topped with a thin layer of unreasonable hope. Mostly she wanted to come up with a good excuse, any excuse, to escape Kate's big makeover plan. To her relief, Kate turned her attention back to Dad. As they discussed the boring details of their wedding plans—how they needed to sell their homes, how Kate needed the summer to finish her job, how they needed a time frame for relocating to San Jose, and other miscellaneous plans for the future—Chelsea mentally checked out. She wished she'd brought a book along.

After dinner, Dad drove Kate to her condo, where he walked her to her door and remained there for exactly seventeen minutes. As Chelsea waited, watching the clock on the console, she wondered what could actually transpire in seventeen minutes . . . or perhaps she didn't really want to know.

"Kate said she'll pick you up at ten tomorrow morning," Dad said as he pulled out of the parking lot.

"Oh, I can hardly wait." She folded her arms tightly across her front, glowering at the street ahead.

"She just wants to help, Chels."

"She wants to make me over, Dad. What does that mean? That I'm not good enough as is?"

"Of course you're good enough as is. You're perfect, honey. You're smart and kind and generous and thoughtful and—"

"Just not pretty."

"I never said that!" He glanced at her. "I think you're very pretty. Your eyes, your bone structure, your mouth. Really, you've got a lot going on that you don't even know about. You're just not one of those shallow foo-foo girls—"

"You mean like Kate?"

"Kate's not like that."

"Yeah, right." She turned away so he couldn't see her eyes rolling.

"She's not like that, Chelsea."

"If you say so, Dad."

"She's really not. You just don't know her well enough yet."

"Right."

"I'll admit that Kate likes fashion and all that sort of thing, but she's not shallow or superficial."

Chelsea knew enough to keep quiet by now.

"And Kate's offer to help you is simply her way of reaching out to you. Naturally, she assumes you'd appreciate some, uh, help. But if you don't want to go with her tomorrow, I'm sure she'll understand. Just call her when we get home. Be honest and tell her that it's not your thing. No one wants to push you into something that's not you. In fact, I think it's rather admirable that you're not into your appearance like that, Chelsea. It shows substance of character."

Chelsea wondered if her dad was simply trying to use reverse psychology. It might've worked when she was thirteen . . . not so much now.

"You have to be yourself, Chels." He continued with his platitudes. "Don't conform to others. And never ever let anyone force you into their cookie-cutter mold."

"You mean like Kate is trying to do?"

"I honestly don't think Kate's trying to do that, honey.

I think she simply sees you as a bit, well, insecure in your appearance. She just wants to help you get over it. But it's obvious that she's stepped over some sort of line." He glanced at her. "In fact, if you like, I'll call Kate myself and tell her that you've changed your mind."

"*Changed* my mind?" she asked. "That would infer that I had something to do with the decision in the first place. As I recall, I was kind of railroaded into the whole make-over plan."

"Exactly." He nodded. "And that's why I'll call Kate and explain that it's not such a good idea." He reached over and patted her knee in a patronizing way. "It's too much too soon. Besides, I almost forgot, I planned to get a head start on packing. I wanted to go over and pick up some moving boxes tomorrow, and then I want us to get started on the garage. It's such a disaster area, I'm sure it'll take us two weeks to get it all sifted down and packed—"

"I know what you're doing, Dad." She let out a loud, exasperated sigh. "Fine, I'll go shopping with Kate."

"Huh?" He looked at her with a surprised expression. "I thought you didn't want to—"

"I *don't* want to. It's just the lesser of two evils."

Neither of them said anything for a while. Chelsea was feeling a little guilty for acting like such a spoiled brat, so finally she broke the silence. "I'm curious about something, Dad."

"Yeah?"

"What made you fall in love with Kate? Was it because she's so beautiful?"

He didn't say anything.

"It was, wasn't it? Kate caught your eye and you just couldn't help yourself, right?"

"Wrong." He shook his head. "That's not how it happened at all."

"Right. I'm sure you didn't even notice that Kate is gorgeous."

"I didn't mean it like that. Of course I noticed her. How could I not? I'm sure she caught my eye when she started working for the corporation last fall."

"You've known her since last fall?"

"Only professionally. And the truth is I assumed Kate was an airhead at first."

"An airhead?"

He nodded. "Yep. She just seemed too doggone pretty to be able to manage a store. In fact, I even questioned Brad in personnel about hiring her. But he showed me her résumé, and it was impressive. Then I saw Kate in action. I saw the way she worked and interacted with people, and I realized I'd completely misjudged her. She's smart and thoughtful and kind." He glanced at Chelsea. "It really is unfair to judge people based on appearances, don't you think?"

She let out a loud, nasal sigh, her new substitute for "duh."

"Anyway, despite knowing there was more to Kate than I originally assumed, I was still uncomfortable with her looks."

"What do you mean?"

"I mean she was just too beautiful. I'd see other guys gaping at her or fawning over her . . . and it was too weird. I knew I couldn't handle it. So I stayed away."

"You're telling me you stayed away from her because you didn't want to be involved with someone that beautiful?" Chelsea was trying to grasp this. Didn't all guys secretly long for a gorgeous woman on their arm? Wrist candy?

"Like I said, it made me uncomfortable. Anyway, for a long time I kept a safe distance from her, if you know what

I mean. I'd actually see her coming from one way and I'd go the other way just to avoid her."

"Why?"

"Several reasons, probably." He pulled into their driveway. "For starters, I figured she'd never give someone like me a second glance. Plus she was younger. You know she's nearly ten years younger than me, but I thought the difference was even greater. So in my thinking, she was out of my league. Too pretty, too young."

"Oh, Dad." Chelsea just shook her head as they got out of the car. "You're pretty cool for an old dude."

"Thanks, sweetie." He put his arm around her as they walked to the front door. "But besides my personal insecurities, I just didn't like the idea of getting involved with someone that . . . that beautiful. It just felt wrong." He unlocked the door, waiting for Chelsea to go inside.

"Why did it feel wrong?" she asked.

"It doesn't make sense now, but I guess I felt like it would make me shallow or superficial." He tossed his car keys into the wooden bowl by the door. "Besides that, Kate was still working for the company back then. That alone should've been enough to scare me off."

"So how did you two ever get together then?"

"Kate would be her usual friendly, outgoing self, and she just started talking to me. I'd be doing a walk-through in the store or checking on something, and she'd come up and just start talking to me like we were old friends. After a while, I began to wish that we were."

"Were what?"

"Old friends." He sat down in his favorite chair. "So I asked her out for coffee one day, and we just seemed to hit it off." He picked up the TV remote. "I suppose the rest is history."

"One more question." Chelsea hesitated.

"Go for it."

"What if Kate *hadn't* been beautiful?"

"What do you mean?"

"Would you have fallen in love with her if she'd been ugly . . . or plain . . . or just plain ugly?"

Dad's brow creased as if he were seriously considering his answer. "It's hard to say, Chelsea. I mean, that's like saying, 'What if Kate was someone else?' How do you answer that? To be honest, I like that Kate's beautiful. I do now anyway. But for the sake of conversation, let's say something happened to her and she lost her looks."

"Okay." Chelsea watched him closely.

Dad leaned his head back, looking up at the ceiling as though thinking hard. He smiled in a slightly dreamy way. "The truth is I would still love her just as much . . . maybe even more."

"Oh."

"Any more questions?"

"No." She shook her head. "Thanks, Dad."

"Want to watch something?" He held up the remote.

"Not tonight." It wasn't even ten yet, but she feigned a yawn. "I'm kind of sleepy."

"Okay." He turned back to the TV, and she went to her room, closing the door quietly behind her. Then she stood in front of the full-length mirror on the back of her door. Her mom had hung that mirror when Chelsea was going into first grade. The plan had been to help Chelsea in coordinating her outfits better. Apparently Chelsea had been just as fashion-challenged then as she was now. Eventually, Mom had taken to arranging Chelsea's outfits for her. Chelsea never minded. She knew some of her friends argued with their moms about clothes, but Chelsea had instinctively known that her mom's sense of style was superior to her own. After Mom died, Chelsea's appearance had gone steadily downhill.

"Don't worry," she told her pathetic-looking image, "*you* will never be loved for your looks." No, Chelsea was certain she'd never have to second-guess whether a guy was interested in her for the wrong thing. Like a guy would ever be interested in her for anything. Well, except for help with his chemistry or calculus. But she was even pretty good at getting out of that.

Chelsea tried to see herself as Kate saw her tonight. What made Kate think that there was any hope of changing anything? Chelsea stared at her muddy-brown hair. She'd been trying to grow it out, thinking that if it was long enough to pull back in a ponytail, that would help somehow. But once it got long enough, all she could do was comb the mousy, frizzy curls as straight as possible and tie them back into a tail that looked more like a frazzled mop than anything. But at least it was out of her face. Not that she particularly enjoyed having her face in full view. Although her braces had been gone for more than a year now, her skin still broke out with unsettling regularity.

In disgust, she turned away from her reflection. It wasn't something she would ever confess to anyone, but Chelsea could relate to Dracula—she hated mirrors!

three

It didn't take long for Chelsea to see that Kate approached shopping like a sport—make that a marathon. Chelsea should've suspected something when Kate handed her a water bottle on their way to the outlet store. "What's this for?"

"Hydration," Kate told her.

"Yes, I understand that concept. But why?"

"Water is good for you, Chelsea. And you're going to need to be hydrated today." Kate studied Chelsea's outfit, which was simply cargo pants, a T-shirt, and flip-flops. "Good choice of clothes," Kate said as she started her car.

"Really?" Chelsea experienced a tinge of hope. "You like it?"

"Not especially." Kate laughed. "No offense. I mean, it's not a very flattering look. But I do like that it'll be easy to get in and out of. You'll be doing a lot of trying on today."

As it turned out, that was putting it mildly. Chelsea's best estimate was that by the end of the day, she had tried on about two hundred items of clothing. She didn't even think that was much of an exaggeration. "That seems like an awful lot of work for just a couple of bags of clothes," she told Kate as they loaded the bags into the car.

"Oh, this was just the beginning."

Chelsea groaned. "I don't want to seem unappreciative, but what else do you think I really need? I mean, I do have more clothes at home, you know."

"I know." Kate's tone suggested that she was unimpressed. "We're going to work on that too."

"I don't really see the point." Chelsea sighed loudly. "I mean, you can dress me differently, but I'm still the same girl underneath."

"Of course you'll be the same girl on the inside," Kate said. "That's the best part of you anyway."

"Really?" Chelsea brightened.

"Absolutely." Kate smiled at her. "But I think your exterior is hurting your interior."

Chelsea didn't say anything.

"The reason I know this is true is because I used to be a lot like you."

"Huh?" Chelsea turned and stared at Kate. "What do you mean exactly?"

"I mean I was an ugly duckling."

"No way."

Kate chuckled. "Way."

"I don't believe you."

"Well, I don't have many photos—because I used to hide every time a camera came out. But I have a few. And if I can dig them out, you'll see that I wore glasses, had braces—"

"I had braces too!"

"I know."

"Dad told you?"

"No, I can tell by your teeth. Like me, you need to use a tooth whitener now."

"Really?" Her hand flew up to her mouth. Now there was something she hadn't even noticed. And that made her wonder—just how bad was she?

"Don't worry, Chelsea." Kate's voice was reassuring. "The good news is that everything that's wrong with you—the outside of you—can be easily fixed."

"Easily fixed?" Chelsea felt seriously skeptical.

"You bet. And I have to say, you've even got more going for you right now than I had when I was your age."

"I need to see those photos."

Kate laughed. "I'll see if I can find them."

"But seriously, how could you possibly have been any, uh, worse-looking than me?" Chelsea felt her face. Just this morning several new zits had appeared.

"I had a bad complexion too," Kate said. "But I found this really great product that's still on the market. I swear that alone changed my life. And I've already ordered you some."

"Really?" Chelsea felt a wave of hope. "And it works?"

"It did for me." She glanced at Chelsea. "I'm sure it'll work for you too. And the other thing you have going for you is your figure."

"My figure?" Chelsea looked down at herself. She'd finally gotten breasts just last year, but now she didn't even know what to do with them. Compared to other girls, it seemed like too little too late.

"Your figure is perfect, Chelsea. But you do need some new underwear—specifically some good bras. Seriously, where did you get the stuff you're wearing?"

Chelsea felt her cheeks grow warm. "I don't know . . . Penney's, I think."

"Well, we're going to address that too." Kate started talking about Brazilian hair-straightening procedures and spray-on tans and French manicures and pedicures and exfoliating facials . . . and Chelsea felt like she was in way over her head.

She held up her hands as Kate pulled up to Chelsea's house. "I'm not sure what all you're talking about, Kate. But I've made a decision."

Kate looked concerned. "You're not chickening out, are you?"

Chelsea shook her head. "No, I'm taking a leap of faith."

"A leap of faith?"

"I'm putting myself in your hands."

Kate broke into a huge grin. "Oh, Chelsea, you won't be sorry. I promise."

Chelsea nodded. "Well, it occurred to me that you can't do any worse than I've done. Any improvement is probably worthwhile. And don't worry, I don't expect miracles."

Kate threw back her head and laughed. "Well, you should. Trust me, you're going to see miracles."

Chelsea knew better than to get her hopes up, but Kate's enthusiasm was contagious. When Kate grabbed one of the clothing bags and followed Chelsea into the house, casually informing her that she was fixing dinner for the three of them tonight, Chelsea was surprised to realize that she was actually sort of glad about this. Was it possible that she was beginning to like Kate?

"I think you should give your dad a fashion show," Kate told Chelsea as they were finishing up dinner.

Dad nodded. "I'd love to see what you girls got."

Chelsea frowned at him. "I don't think so."

Kate looked disappointed as she began to clear the table.

"The clothes are all nice and everything." Chelsea stood too, picking up her plate and the salad bowl. "It's just that I'm not ready to put them all on again. Okay?" She forced a smile. "How about if I clean this up and you guys can go relax?"

Dad grinned. "You talked me into it."

"How about an after-dinner walk?" Kate suggested.

With Dad and Kate gone, Chelsea cranked up the music and put kitchen cleaning into high gear. She'd been surprised to see that Kate was a fairly good cook. Of course, anyone could make spaghetti. But it was somewhat reassuring to know that Kate knew her way around a kitchen. It helped to erase the wicked stepmother image.

Chelsea was just heading to her room when Dad and Kate returned from their walk. "Hey, Chels," Kate called out. "How about if we take that inventory of your closet now?"

Chelsea wanted to say, "Thanks, but no thanks," but Kate looked so hopeful as she hurried to catch up with her.

"If you clean stuff out now, it'll make it that much easier to pack it up when moving time comes."

"I guess." Chelsea cautiously opened the door to her room. "It's just that it's kind of messy in here and—"

"Oh, don't worry about that. I used to be a total slob. I doubt you can surprise me much." Kate headed directly for Chelsea's closet.

As if today hadn't been hard enough—trying on outfit after outfit and being scrutinized again and again—letting anyone (especially perfect Kate) look in her closet was way beyond Chelsea's comfort zone. Still, she was determined to cooperate. She understood that Kate was simply trying to help, and on some levels Chelsea did appreciate it. Pressing her lips together, she sat on the edge of her bed, watching as Kate removed an armful of clothes and flopped them down on the bed next to Chelsea.

"Okay, this has got to go." Kate held up a ratty-looking sweatshirt.

Chelsea felt a small wave of regret. That sweatshirt had always felt so nice and loose and comfortable.

"Come on," Kate urged. "You might as well wear a potato sack as this."

"Okay."

Kate tossed the shirt to the floor. "This will be the cast-off pile." She held up a pair of flared jeans. "These are so last year, Chelsea." She threw them on top of the sweatshirt, and Chelsea controlled herself from snatching them back.

"Now this has potential." Kate held up a plain white shirt. "Nice lines."

Chelsea frowned at the top. "I had to get that when I was a freshman, because I was in choir and we had to wear white blouses with navy skirts."

"Does it still fit?"

Chelsea shrugged.

"Come on." Kate handed her the shirt. "Try it."

While Chelsea was trying on the shirt, Kate continued thinning Chelsea's closet. The white shirt as well as some sweaters and a few other basic pieces wound up being keepers, but the cast-off pile looked enormous.

"Are you sure about that?" Chelsea pointed to the mountain of old clothes. "I mean, what am I supposed to wear?"

"Don't forget about these." Kate went over to the door,

where Chelsea had dropped her bags of clothing. "Let's hang them up and then we'll make a list."

"A list?" Chelsea picked up a bag and emptied the contents onto her bed.

"Sure. We'll see what you have and I can figure out what you'll need."

After they hung up the clothes and Kate had arranged everything in the closet, Chelsea had to admit that it did look better. As Kate combined pieces, showing Chelsea what went with what, Chelsea could almost imagine becoming somewhat stylish. At least more stylish than she'd ever been before.

"You make it look easy," Chelsea told Kate. "But when I try to put stuff together, it doesn't work. I just end up looking lame."

"I have a plan for that too." Kate smiled knowingly. "Trust me, okay?"

Chelsea just nodded.

"You still need a lot of things, including shoes and a couple of perfect pairs of jeans, and that will take some time," Kate said, making a list. "And you need some good accessories—belts and bags and those touches that take clothes from being garments to being fashions."

"How did you learn all this?"

Kate laughed. "I've been working in retail clothing stores for years, Chelsea. After a while, it just comes naturally."

Chelsea felt pretty sure it would never come naturally to her.

"We'll do some more shopping next weekend," Kate said, "and next week I'll make you a hair appointment. And, well, some other things too." She smiled. "By the time you and your dad move to San Jose, you will look like a whole new person."

"I'm curious . . ." Chelsea began.

"About what?"

Chelsea questioned the sensibility of asking her question. Except that she wanted to know. "Why are you doing this?"

"Doing what specifically?"

"Being so helpful with this whole makeover business." Chelsea watched Kate's expression carefully.

Kate looked slightly confused. "Do you feel like I'm interfering? Or being too pushy? I know I can be kind of bossy. I hope I haven't offended you by taking over and—"

"No, that's not it." Chelsea stood, forcing herself to look at her reflection in the mirror again. Two days in a row was a record for her. "I mean, why are you so obsessed with this makeover? Is it because you're embarrassed that I'll be your stepdaughter?"

"No, of course not." Kate stood next to Chelsea, putting an arm around her. "It's simply because I care about you. And like I said, I can relate to you. Wait until I find those photos, Chelsea. Then you'll get it."

Chelsea felt tears in her eyes, and she wasn't even sure why. "I'll never be as beautiful as you, Kate. It's not even possible."

Kate laughed. "Don't be so sure." She started doing an inventory on Chelsea. "You and your dad both have the most gorgeous brown eyes. And once we get those brows plucked—professionally—your eyes will be even prettier. And your nose is absolutely perfect."

"You mean besides that zit?"

Kate laughed again. "You're just seeing it all wrong. Your lips are nice and full." She pointed to her own mouth. "I have to do all kinds of lip-liner tricks to make my lips look like that. All you'll need is some lip gloss." She went on talking about how Chelsea's figure was so good. "If you worked out a little, it would probably be flawless. And once we get you wearing the right clothes, people will actually see how great it is."

Chelsea frowned. She wasn't sure she wanted anyone to see her figure. She'd gotten so used to covering herself up . . . the idea of being visible and exposed was pretty scary.

"Anyway, don't worry about it, okay?" Kate patted Chelsea's cheek. "You're on the cusp of becoming as beautiful on the outside as you are on the inside. Just think of it, you'll be going to a new school this fall, and who knows how great your last two years of high school might be."

Chelsea smiled weakly. As much as she wanted to believe that what Kate was saying could be possible, she remembered that old saying—if something seemed too good to be true, it probably was. Also, she knew from experience that she was foolish to get her hopes up. Mostly she just wanted to humor Kate. It was sweet that Kate cared this much. Hopefully she wouldn't be too disappointed either.

four

Kate kept her promise of scheduling all kinds of appointments and treatments for Chelsea's magical makeover plan. The next few weeks passed in a kind of surreal swirl of beauty procedures and fashion-focused fittings. Chelsea tried to cooperate with Kate's plans, but there were moments, like the eyebrow "threading" session, when she totally lost it and jumped right out of the chair.

"You want have unibrow?" the Nazi-like woman demanded in her thick east-European accent. She hovered near Chelsea with this string device that was somehow removing hairs one at a time.

Chelsea rubbed her throbbing brow line. "I would like *some* eyebrows left behind."

The woman laughed in a mean way. "Don't worry. You have enough eyebrows for five or six girls. Now you want me continue or not?"

Chelsea hesitantly climbed back into the chair.

"Is the price we pay for beauty," the woman said in a slightly gentler tone. "You will see."

Chelsea had reason to trust Kate's guidance in these matters, because to her utter amazement, Kate's "secret remedy" for clear skin was actually beginning to work. Chelsea's complexion had never looked better.

"It hasn't even been three weeks since I started using it, but that acne stuff is really working," Chelsea told Kate as they were driving through town. She touched her cheek, still amazed that she hadn't had a recent breakout. "I mean, I'd seen the ads on TV, you know the ones with the before and after photos, but I figured it was just a hoax. Like how could anything work like that?"

"Well, it probably doesn't work like that for everyone. But it worked for me, and it obviously is for you too. Just remember that the secret to a good complexion includes a number of things." Kate nodded at Chelsea. "Including keeping your hands off your face."

Chelsea put her hand in her lap.

"Cleaning your skin properly is important too. But so is eating right. And drinking water is vital."

It was the Saturday before Chelsea and Dad would be moving to San Jose. Today they were on their way to the much-anticipated hair and makeup appointment. Kate was calling this the Big Reveal day. Following their visit to Kate's salon, where they both had appointments, they planned to go back home, dress up, and meet Dad downtown for dinner.

"Now, you're sure you want to lighten your hair?" Kate asked Chelsea again. "I'd hate to think I influenced you on this. The straightening process alone will make a huge difference."

"I read that the Brazilian Blowout works better on processed and frizzy hair," Chelsea reminded her. "My hair's frizzy enough, but it's never been processed."

"That's true."

"So I think I want the whole works." Chelsea nodded. "Unless you think it won't look good?" She was second-guessing herself again.

"No, I totally think it'll look good. I just want it to be your decision, Chelsea. Not mine."

Chelsea nodded again. "It is my decision."

"All right."

Chelsea felt nervous as they went into the salon, but it wasn't exactly a bad kind of nervous. More like giddy. This whole makeover business had really been growing on her lately. Probably because she had finally started to see some results. The eyebrow thinning had actually been a huge improvement, and the clearing complexion was monumental. Also, she'd been doing the exercise DVD that Kate had given her, as well as using a faux tan product. That was a mess the first time, but after she learned to exfoliate and do some other tricks, it got easier. Now she didn't even feel embarrassed to wear a sleeveless top and a skirt—pieces that Kate had picked out. And with her recent manicure and pedicure, she didn't mind having her bare toes showing in the new pair of sandals that Kate had encouraged her to get.

"This will eventually stop costing me money, right?" Dad had commented a few days ago. He hadn't known that Chelsea was within earshot as he made his complaints to his fiancée. "I just got the bill from the store, and despite the discount, it was a little surprising. Now you're doing all these beauty treatments too."

"Hey, Alex, you've gotten off pretty easy these past few years," Kate said in a slightly scolding tone. "I saw Chelsea's closet, so I know what I'm talking about. Even if it costs you a little more now, you should be thankful for Chelsea's sake. You might've saved some money, but it was all at your daughter's expense."

Then it had gotten quiet in the kitchen, and Chelsea suspected that Kate had sweetened her chastisement with a kiss or two. Really, Kate was spot-on. Dad had gotten off cheap since Mom died. Chelsea rarely asked him for a penny when it came to clothes or makeup or anything to do with appearances. In fact, he had usually been the one to nag her to buy a new dress or something. So, she decided, she was not going to start feeling guilty now.

Kate was involved in the initial consultation regarding the correct shade of blonde and how much highlighting seemed best for Chelsea. And Chelsea, like she'd been doing for weeks now, simply trusted Kate's judgment on this. While the beautician, a pretty brunette named Andrea, applied foil and goopy stuff, Chelsea simply daydreamed.

She imagined herself finally looking like the other girls— the ones who'd left her in their dust. She imagined herself going up to Virginia and saying, "What do you think of me now?" Although she knew she'd never do that for real. Not only would it be humiliating, it would be pointless. And what if Virginia laughed at her? Or told Chelsea that she still didn't measure up? No, she didn't need that. Kate had been giving her little speeches about believing in herself, about holding her head high, about acting like she was equal to anyone. Chelsea supposed she believed that, at least on most levels—intellectually, morally, inwardly. It was just those exterior things that got her down.

"I don't want to see my hair until you're completely done," Chelsea told Andrea as she closed her eyes. "Is that okay?"

Andrea chuckled. "Yeah, it's fine. It'll be fun to see your reaction. Kind of like how they do it on *What Not to Wear*."

While more steps of varying procedures were performed on Chelsea's hair, she kept her eyes closed or away from the mirror until finally the blow-dryer stopped.

"Okay," Andrea said. "All done."

Chelsea opened her eyes and was shocked to see a gorgeous head of silky blonde hair. She gave her head a shake and realized that her hair actually swung and moved. It was cut in layers, with the longest part just a couple of inches below her shoulders. She fingered it. "I didn't even know my hair was this long."

"It always gets longer when it's straightened." Andrea smiled. "Do you like it?"

"No." Chelsea shook her head again. "I *love* it!"

Kate joined them. "Oh, Chelsea," she gushed. "It looks amazing."

Chelsea was still touching it. "I can't believe this is really my hair. It feels totally different."

"It's yours," Andrea told her. "You're lucky that it's nice and thick. Some girls get the blowout and discover their hair is too thin."

"How often will she need to have this done?" Kate asked.

"About eight to ten weeks." Andrea showed them some hair products. "If you use these, it will last longer and really improve the quality of your hair."

Kate touched Chelsea's hair. "And it's true that her hair will stay straight and smooth even if she goes swimming?"

Andrea nodded. "Even in the ocean."

"Amazing."

Chelsea was so happy she hugged both Kate and Andrea. "I feel like a different person," she told them. She was still shaking her head, enjoying the feel of the silky hair on her bare shoulders. It really was amazing.

"We're not done yet," Kate reminded her. They went over to another station. "Leanne is a cosmetologist," Kate told Chelsea after she introduced her. "She's going to help you learn the basics of makeup."

"Have you used makeup before?" Leanne asked.

"I tried a couple of times, but I looked like a clown. So I gave up."

"Well, you don't need to look like a clown," Leanne assured her. "We'll go for a natural look, okay?" She showed Chelsea some powders that she called minerals, and step-by-step she showed Chelsea how brushes were used and how the colors were layered on to look natural. "They're actually good for your skin," she told her. "You can even sleep in them if you want."

"But don't," Kate said. "You need to keep up your skin-care routine if you want to keep your complexion clear."

Leanne showed Chelsea how to use an eyeliner pencil and how to smudge it with her fingertip so it didn't look too dramatic. She also showed her how to use eye shadow. "Just for fun," she said. Finally she showed her how to use mascara and lip color. "And that's all there is to it." She turned the chair around so Chelsea could see in the mirror.

"Wow!" Chelsea leaned forward, staring in wonder. "It's like someone else."

"Are you okay with it?" Leanne sounded worried.

"Absolutely." Chelsea looked at Kate. "Do you think Dad will mind if I get some of these products too?"

"This one is on me, Chels." Kate nodded at Leanne. "We'll take some of everything that you used on her today."

As they were driving home, Chelsea confessed to Kate about how she used to relate to Dracula.

"Dracula?" Kate frowned. "Was he a vampire or a werewolf or what? I don't exactly recall."

"Vampire."

"Oh, like the Twilight books?"

"Sort of. But Bram Stoker wrote *Dracula* more than a hundred years ago. In Stoker's novel, a vampire couldn't see his reflection in a mirror, so he had to avoid mirrors."

"I don't get it. I mean, what difference would it make?"

"A vampire wouldn't want anyone to see him looking in a mirror," Chelsea explained, "because he wouldn't be visible and then they'd know he was a vampire. So he just steered clear of mirrors."

"Right." Kate frowned. "I'm sorry . . . I'm still kind of lost."

"Well, that's what I'd tell myself—that I couldn't look in the mirror either. The truth was I'd get so depressed every time I looked in the mirror that I'd feel like jumping off a bridge or something. So I just avoided mirrors altogether."

"Oh, Chelsea." Kate shook her head. "I'm so sorry."

"It's okay." Chelsea smiled. "I have a feeling those days are behind me now."

"I hope so."

It seemed those days really were a thing of the past as Chelsea dressed for their Big Reveal dinner. After she'd put on the periwinkle-blue BCBG sundress with the thin belt that matched the bronze sandals, she couldn't stop staring at herself in the full-length mirror. Even though she felt a little foolish, not to mention vain, she couldn't stop looking. She'd pose from all angles and even practice walking since heels were still new to her, but she simply couldn't believe her eyes.

"Are you ready?" Kate asked as she knocked on the bedroom door.

"I guess so." Still she stood gaping at herself.

Kate opened the door, causing the mirror to angle away from Chelsea so that she was just standing there. "Oh my!" Kate grinned. "You are a knockout, Chelsea. A totally hot knockout."

"I, uh, I think I'm in shock," Chelsea admitted. "Maybe it's kind of like culture shock."

"Yes, it will take some getting used to. To be honest, my transformation, back when I was your age, happened a little more slowly. But that's because I didn't have help."

Chelsea felt her eyes filling with tears. "Oh, Kate!" She threw her arms around her. "I was worried that you were going to be a wicked stepmother, but it's like you're really a fairy godmother instead." Chelsea went over to her dresser and picked up the framed photo of her mom. She held it out as if her mom could peer at her from the photo. "I know if Mom could see me now, if she could see how you've helped me . . . well, she would love you too."

Now they were both crying. Hugging and crying. Then they had to fix their eye makeup again and retouch their lip gloss.

"Okay, gorgeous girl." Kate grinned at her. "Ready to go make an appearance?"

Chelsea nodded. "Dad's probably already there waiting for us."

"I told him to be patient." Kate looked at the purses that Chelsea had laid on her bed. "This one," she told her, picking up the ivory Kate Spade bag. "Perfect."

Chelsea wasn't surprised when Dad nearly fell out of his chair to see them coming his way. "You've got to be kidding," he told them. "This is someone else you've brought with you, Kate. This cannot be my daughter."

Chelsea gave a mock frown. "Are you saying I don't look good?"

He shook his head. "No, sweetie, you look incredible. I just can't believe it's really you." He stared at her. "I always knew you were beautiful, but I've never seen you this put together."

Chelsea grinned at Kate. "Thanks to Kate."

Dad pulled out Kate's chair, and before he could pull out Chelsea's chair, the waiter stepped in. "Here, let me help the lovely young lady," he said with an approving expression.

Even though this was the same restaurant they'd eaten at more than a month ago, and it was even the same waiter, Chelsea felt like she was truly someone else. Before, she'd felt invisible . . . or worse. But tonight she not only felt visible, she felt pretty and appreciated.

Okay, she realized that it seemed a little weird, maybe even wrong, to suddenly feel appreciated simply because she'd changed her exterior appearance. But just the same, she liked it. Did that make her shallow or superficial? Did it mean she was a fake, a phony? After all, hadn't she thought those same things, passed those same judgments on some of her old friends—including Virginia? What if she had turned into one of them?

No, of course not, she reassured herself. She was still Chelsea Martin. After those horrible years of being put down and picked on thanks to her looks, she knew she would never act that way to anyone. Never! She would rather turn back into her plain ugly self than turn into a mean girl. If nothing else, she had learned the hard way what it felt like to be snubbed for her looks. She would never go there—no matter what, she would never stoop that low. She knew better than anyone that beneath this polished veneer, she was still the same vulnerable girl. She knew what it felt like to hurt. She also knew that her own deep insecurities, unlike her exterior appearance, would be slow to change. Perhaps that was for the best.

five

Thanks to a reduced price on their house, the sale closed just days before they were scheduled to leave. Already Dad had a Realtor lined up to show them a dozen houses in their price range in a subdivision not far from where he'd be working in San Jose.

Today was the big day. The big truck with a huge storage pod had just left. Completely loaded with all their things, it was now on its way to a site where the pod would sit until they were ready to have it shipped to San Jose. Dad and Chelsea would've been on the road too, but Kate had stopped by on her way to work to say goodbye.

"I can't believe this won't be home anymore," Chelsea said to Dad as they did one last walk around the yard.

He nodded. "I know what you mean."

"I can't believe you're really going to drive all the way out there," Kate said. "You could've flown and had the car shipped."

"I've always wanted to take a cross-country trip," he said. "I had the vacation time coming anyway."

"And we'll take turns driving," Chelsea pointed out. "That way I'll have enough driving hours to apply for my license when we get to California."

Dad frowned. "We'll see about that."

"I'm going to miss you both so much," Kate said as she hugged them.

"Then hurry and sell your condo and come out and join us," Chelsea urged her.

"I wish I could." Kate shook her head. "But you know I promised to stay at my job until the end of September."

"It's going to be a long two months." Dad sighed.

"Well, at least I'll have the wedding plans to keep me busy."

"And I already booked our flight back here," he added.

"Thank goodness for Skype," she said. "We can talk face-to-face every night."

"And maybe I can talk you into flying out," he said. "Maybe for Labor Day weekend?"

"We'll see."

Chelsea turned away while they embraced and kissed. As much as she was used to Kate by now, she was still not used to seeing them kissing. But at least she wasn't saying "eeuw."

"Well, we better hit the road if we're going to make Topeka by this evening."

Kate shook her head. "That's a lot of driving for one day. You two better be careful."

"We will."

"Oh, I almost forgot something." Kate ran back to her car, returning with a small paper bag and something else. "This is for you, Chelsea." She winked as she handed her the bag. "Hopefully they'll fit."

Chelsea peeked inside the bag. "What is it?"

"You said you didn't have a swimsuit. I figured you'd be stopping at some hotels with pools, so I picked up a couple of suits for you."

"Thanks!" Chelsea hugged her again. "By the way, do you still want me to be in your wedding?"

"Of course I do. I thought we'd been over all that by now."

"Oh, okay."

Kate put her hand on Chelsea's cheek. "I'm going to miss you, sweetie."

"I'm going to miss you too."

Kate handed Dad a CD. "Something for the road."

"Dionne Warwick?" Dad cocked his head to one side. "Huh?"

"Song number six." She grinned. "Just listen."

They were about ten minutes out of town when song number six came on. They both laughed to hear "Do You Know the Way to San Jose?" Chelsea turned the volume up, trying to understand the lyrics.

"I don't know if I ever heard Dionne Warwick before, but I actually like her," Chelsea said after the CD ended.

"I've got an idea," Dad said. "What if you and I memorize the lyrics to the San Jose song and we can do a duet for Kate at the wedding reception?"

Chelsea's first reaction was to say forget it. But remembering how much Kate had done for her, and knowing that she should no longer have such a phobia about being in front of people, she agreed.

They took turns driving, and finally at a little past seven

they made it to Topeka. After a quick fast-food dinner, they checked into a motel. Seeing that there was a rather inviting-looking pool next to the lobby, Chelsea decided to try out one of the swimsuits Kate had given her. When she pulled them out of the bag, she was surprised to see how skimpy they both were. One was actually a string bikini. The other had a little more coverage but was still beyond Chelsea's comfort zone. But seeing her dad crashing on one of the beds and tuning into a sports network, she decided to go for it. After all, it was a hot summer night and she didn't know a soul in this town. What did she have to lose?

She went into the bathroom and put on the swimsuit with more coverage, then just stared at her image in the mirror. With her faux tan and lightened and straightened hair, plus the other improvements, she really didn't recognize this girl. She admired herself from various angles, and feeling surprisingly confident, albeit a little nervous, she wrapped a towel around her like a sarong skirt and slipped out. Dad was already snoring, so she left him a note saying she'd be at the pool. She rode the elevator down and got a soda from the machine, then ventured out to the pool area.

Several teens as well as some younger kids were noisily enjoying the pool, and Chelsea was barely in the area before she began to feel extremely awkward and self-conscious. She noticed a couple of the teens glancing her way, probably taking inventory. Suddenly she knew there was no way she was going to remove her sarong towel and get into the pool. But she felt too embarrassed to turn and leave.

Trying to appear nonchalant, she pulled a table next to a lounge chair and set her soda down. She wanted to look comfortable in her own skin as she sat down, but she knew this was a joke. Anyone with eyes in their head could see through this pathetic act. Chelsea felt like a fish out of water.

She took a deep breath, something Kate had told her to do, and began to remind herself of some of the little confidence-instilling tricks Kate had been trying to teach her.

"Smile," she had told Chelsea again and again. "It not only increases your face value, it makes you feel better inwardly. And when you feel better on the inside, it radiates to the outside."

Although she'd been a skeptic at first, Chelsea knew from trying this little smiling trick that it really was true. She did feel better when she smiled. It's like it changed something inside of her. Usually anyway. At the moment it felt silly to sit there smiling. Too bad she hadn't brought a book or a magazine with her. Then she could've pretended to be highly amused by what she was reading.

She moved on to another Kate tip. "Make eye contact with the person who's intimidating you." How was she supposed to do that when there were five teens—two guys and three girls—making her uncomfortable? Not that they were saying anything, but she felt their glances. After years of practicing avoidance and playing the wallflower, she found that looking away came very naturally. Seriously, how was she supposed to make eye contact? Not only did it feel personally threatening, it was downright scary. Even so, she made a couple of feeble attempts. She wondered if Kate would be laughing at her right now. But it was just too hard. How was she supposed to make eye contact with a perfect stranger? Furthermore, why should she even want to?

She leaned back in the lounge and gazed at the fogged-up roof covering the pool, recalling something else Kate had told her—something Kate had said quite often. "You need to change your interior dialogue." At first Chelsea hadn't understood how that was even possible, but Kate had made her practice by saying the words aloud. Like a parrot, Chelsea would repeat them after Kate. Now she recited them inside her head. *I am an attractive, intelligent girl. I have a lot to offer other people. People want to get to know me.*

"Hey," a guy said to her.

She turned to see a guy with dark hair standing next to her lounge chair, looking down at her. He was smiling, and she realized he was even better looking up close than from a distance. That alone made her want to freeze or run the other way. Then she remembered Kate's advice. *Smile.* So she forced a smile. *Make eye contact.* She did that too.

"Hey what?" she asked him in a voice that sounded somewhat like her own.

"Are you afraid of the water or something?"

She glanced over to the pool, then forced another smile as well as a shrug. "Looks a little crowded in there," she managed to say. Her throat felt dry and she felt shaky inside. This was so out of her comfort zone.

"So how about the Jacuzzi?" He nodded to the hot tub at the end of the pool, where one of the teen girls was sitting.

"Oh." She nodded, reaching for her soda, wanting something wet to coat her throat. "I hadn't thought of that."

"Well, you should." He grinned at her. "There's room for everyone."

She took a sip of soda, then using every ounce of determination, she locked eyes with him. Eye contact. "I guess I'll check it out," she said as evenly as she could. With trembling knees, she stood and slowly removed her towel and started

walking toward the hot tub. Every move she made felt calcu-
lated and careful. This was something else Kate had taught
her. When you feel self-conscious, insecure, or uncomfortable, slow down.

"Whether it's your movements or your words, don't fall
into the speed trap." She had explained that when Chelsea
spoke too quickly or moved too quickly, it sent the message
that she was fearful and anxious. "It sets you up to be a tar-
get," Kate said. "So just slow down. Think and move and
speak carefully. Then you'll sound confident."

Chelsea took a deep breath as she approached the Jacuzzi.
She made eye contact and smiled at the blonde girl in the tub
as she eased herself in. "This feels good," she told her.

"Yeah, it's not bad." The girl smiled back. Chelsea tried not
to act surprised, but she'd been prepared for a snub from the
pretty girl. Instead, she was acting friendly. It seemed that Kate's
tricks really did work. You smiled and made eye contact, and
just like that people were friendly. Who'd've thunk?

The dark-haired guy got into the hot tub too, slipping into
a seat next to Chelsea. "I'm Jake," he told her. He pointed
to the other teen guy, who was coming their way. "That's
my buddy Adam. We're both ball players, and our coach is
taking us to a Royals game tomorrow."

"That's cool." Chelsea nodded, trying to remember all
of Kate's tips.

"Baseball?" the other girl said. "What position do you play?"

Jake turned to her. "Catcher mostly."

"Cool." The girl nodded. "I'm Nora. My older brother
plays college baseball, so I'm kind of into that too. Who are
the Royals playing?"

Jake started to tell her a bit about the team and how he

hoped that he'd be good enough by his senior year to get a college scholarship or even get picked up by a minor league team.

"Wow," Nora said, "you must be good."

Jake shrugged and turned to Chelsea. "So you know our names. How about telling us yours?"

"Sorry." She smiled again. "I'm Chelsea. My dad and I are on a road trip to California."

"California." Jake nodded. "Where 'bouts?"

She explained about the job change and San Jose, and Jake acted as if it were the most interesting topic in the world. Chelsea glanced over to see Nora watching them closely. "How about you?" Chelsea asked her. "What are you doing in Topeka?"

Nora explained that she was on a family vacation. She nodded toward the noisy throng of kids in the pool. "Some of those brats are my siblings." She rolled her eyes. "I'm supposed to be watching them, but I'm secretly hoping they drown."

Jake laughed, and Chelsea imitated him by laughing too. Jake's friend had joined them, and now Chelsea found herself flanked by two very good-looking guys. Nora chatted easily with them, and Chelsea tried to keep up with the friendly banter, hoping that her insecurities would remain at bay. Then a couple of the other teen girls came into the Jacuzzi too.

"It's getting cozy in here." Jake slid closer to Chelsea to make more room.

Chelsea just smiled, continuing her attempt to act natural. The conversation became more animated, and it was clear that the two newcomer girls were flirting with the boys. One of the girls was a little overweight, but she was witty and funny and had the kind of confidence Chelsea was still wishing for.

The other girl was eager to show off a recent tattoo on her lower back.

Still, it seemed clear—although extremely unbelievable—that Jake and Adam were more interested in Chelsea than in the other three girls in the hot tub. Chelsea felt almost giddy at this totally unexpected attention. Here she was sitting in a Jacuzzi with three other girls, whose looks ranged from quite pretty to just okay, and the two guys seemed to be vying for Chelsea's attention. Chelsea Martin had turned not just one guy's head, but two.

Although it was fun and exciting, it was also dizzyingly overwhelming, and at times she felt lost in keeping up with the witty banter. Plus she had occasional flashbacks to times she'd been teased or put down. She wondered if she suffered from some kind of post-traumatic stress disorder. Was it possible that girls who'd been picked on and bullied were similar to soldiers who'd survived combat zones? Really, other than explosives and physical injuries, what was the difference?

"Guess we scared those two away," Nora was saying a bit smugly. Chelsea looked up to see the two newcomer girls exiting the Jacuzzi. Judging by their expressions and demeanor—which were painfully familiar to Chelsea—she thought it was possible that something might've been said to drive them away.

"So what are you into?" Jake asked Chelsea.

She felt stumped. A guy her age had never asked her a question like this. Instead of blurting out something that would forever categorize her as a geek girl, she reminded herself of Kate's "slow down" advice. "Just the usual stuff," she told him. Even though she knew she probably sounded silly and shallow, she started to blab on about a reality show.

Fortunately, they were all familiar with it, and the conversation continued moving along.

"You remind me of Todd Davis," Nora told Adam. It seemed she was focusing all her attention on him, hoping that he'd return the favor. Chelsea knew that Todd Davis was the hottie on the reality show they were currently dissing and discussing.

"Thanks a lot," Adam said. "Todd's a total dork."

Nora laughed. "Yeah, but he's a good-looking dork."

"I think Chelsea looks like that Amanda character," Jake said in a tone that oozed of approval.

"You mean Miranda," Nora corrected. "I don't really think so."

"Amanda, Miranda, whatever." Jake put a finger beneath Chelsea's chin, turning her head as if to study her even more closely.

She controlled herself from cringing or trying to hide, but she couldn't help letting out a nervous giggle. This was so totally weird . . . so unsettling . . . and yet she knew by his expression that he liked her looks and was enjoying himself immensely.

"I think she looks like Cameron Diaz," Adam said as he moved in closer on the other side. "I mean when Cameron was younger. She's like, what, forty now?"

"Yeah. She's old, but she's still hot." Jake nodded. "Yeah, I think you're right. Chelsea does look like a younger Cameron Diaz. Except for the eyes." He looked intently into Chelsea's eyes. "I think Cameron's are blue. But Chelsea's are brown and lots prettier." The expression on his face was almost frightening, like he thought she was a deluxe cheeseburger and he was about to gobble her up.

Nora stood up. "Well, since you two guys are having so much fun at your Chelsea love festival, I think I'll bow out."

"Don't go yet," Chelsea said quickly. "These guys are just teasing me."

Nora's eyes narrowed slightly, but she sat back down.

"You know who Nora looks like?" Chelsea was racking her brain, trying to come up with a believable actress's name.

"Who?" Nora asked.

"Keira Knightley!" Chelsea exclaimed. Okay, she knew that was crazy, but it was the only name that came to her. As she watched the boys looking from Nora to her and then back again, she remembered why that name came to mind. Kate had mentioned that she thought Chelsea looked like Keira.

"No, Nora doesn't look like Keira Knightley," Jake said. "You do."

"I am so outta here." Nora stood again, adjusted her bikini, and, without any protest from the guys, made her exit.

"Now I guess we'll just have to fight over you," Jake said in a teasing tone.

Chelsea laughed nervously.

"So, if you had to choose between us," Adam said enticingly, "who would you choose?" He struck an attractive pose.

Jake pushed his friend on the shoulder, and Adam feigned a fall. "She'd pick me, of course," Jake told him.

Chelsea was feeling more than just a little light-headed now. She was actually dizzy. "I think I need to get out of here," she said as she grabbed the handrail and stood. "I'm feeling kinda fuzzy. I think it's the heat."

Suddenly the two guys were helping her from the Jacuzzi and into the pool. Compared to the heat of the hot tub, the pool felt icy and the shock made her jump. With a pounding heart, she took in a big breath and dove under the water, then swam the length of the pool in an effort to calm herself and put some space between her and the two guys. Back in middle school, she'd been on the swim team and not such a bad swimmer. It felt good to have this kind of control now.

At the end where the younger kids were jumping and yelling and splashing, she quickly turned and swam back to the hot tub area where the guys, who reminded her of hungry sharks, were still waiting for her. She wanted to play this cool, to act like this was nothing out of the ordinary for her, but the truth was, like the water on this end, she was in way over her head.

"You guys are great," she told them in as smooth a voice as she could muster while she used the ladder to climb out of the pool. "But we have to get up really early tomorrow. I'm helping my dad with the driving, and it's getting kind of late."

They protested as they followed her over to get her towel, but she managed to make them see her point. However, they did talk her into giving them her email address. "In case we're ever out in San Jose," Jake told her. But when they asked about Facebook, she pretended not to have a page, saying she thought social networks were lame.

As she returned to the hotel room, feeling like she'd just dodged some sort of bullet, she reminded herself she'd have to remove her Facebook page now. Too bad she'd put it under her own name. But no way did she want anyone to see the phony pics she'd put up. Of course, with her new image, she could put up real photos without embarrassment now.

six

Dad was just emerging from the bathroom when Chelsea returned to their hotel room. Toweling off his damp hair, he was wearing one of the motel bathrobes and had a slightly worried expression. "I was about to come looking for you," he told her.

"Why?" She tightened the towel around her waist, making her way toward the still-steamy bathroom.

He gave a sheepish grin. "I don't know that I'm too comfortable having my drop-dead-gorgeous daughter running around in a strange city all by herself."

"Oh, Dad!" She shook her head like she thought he was crazy. But in reality, she wondered if he might not have a healthier understanding of what had just transpired down at the pool than she did. She considered asking him about it but didn't want to make him any more concerned than he was. This was something she would have to get used to

. . . and learn to handle on her own. "Remember, I'm not a little kid anymore."

He looked doubtful. "I don't know about that, but at least you've got a good head on your shoulders. That's more than a lot of kids your age have." He stifled a yawn. "Don't know about you, but I'm hitting the hay."

She glanced at the clock between the two beds. "It's not even ten yet."

"I know, but I'm beat. Go ahead and turn the TV on if you like, just keep the sound down. Okay?"

"Okay."

After her shower, she flipped on the TV. She knew it was silly, but she wanted to find a movie with Keira Knightley or Cameron Diaz starring. No such luck. She considered digging out her laptop and doing an internet search for photos of the two beauties, but then she realized she was about to cross over from mild curiosity to obsession. She never used to be like this. Who cared who she looked like? As long as she didn't look like the old Chelsea.

As she carefully combed her freshly shampooed and conditioned hair, which was still as smooth and silky as before swimming, she wanted to wrap her head around her new and interesting dilemma. How was a girl supposed to act when guys treated her the way Jake and Adam had tonight? It was a thrill and a rush for sure, but how was a girl like Chelsea ever supposed to get used to that kind of attention? Nothing had prepared her for this.

She came to a movie channel that was playing the Sandra Bullock film *Miss Congeniality*, and although she remembered seeing it a long time ago, before Mom died, she started watching it again. Sandra's situation was different (she was older and playing an FBI agent), but some parts of the movie felt painfully similar. Going from drab to fab didn't come without its own special set of challenges. As she watched Sandra's clumsy pratfalls and corny mishaps, all of which were pretty humorous, Chelsea decided that when they got settled in San Jose and she was going to her new high school, she definitely did not want to end up looking like that kind of a goofball.

It might've made for a humorous movie, but Chelsea had been there, done that. She'd spent way too much time on the losing end of lame jokes and bullying and teasing, and she had no desire to set herself up for more. She realized that if that Jacuzzi scene had lasted any longer, or if Nora or the other girls had stuck around, Chelsea would've eventually stuck her foot in her mouth. Pedicure or not, she would've ended up making a complete fool of herself. It wouldn't have been such a big deal tonight since it was unlikely she'd ever see those kids again. But eventually it could be a big deal.

Her mind was made up. Even if it took a lot of work and preparation, and even if she had to memorize all of Kate's secrets to self-esteem or tattoo CliffsNotes on her palm, Chelsea was determined she would master this. Kate had pulled out all the stops to turn Chelsea into a new person on the outside, and it was up to Chelsea to do all she could to make sure the rest of her matched up.

The next two days passed relatively uneventfully. When Chelsea wasn't behind the wheel, she was studying the notes she'd made based on advice Kate had given her, as well as reading a variety of fluffy fashion and pop culture magazines that she picked up during their meal stops.

"You've been awfully quiet all afternoon," Dad said as

the city of Albuquerque came into view on their third day on the road.

"Sorry," she told him as she closed the magazine.

"Are those, uh, magazines really that interesting?"

She laughed. "Not at first. But I want to try to fit in better, you know? I was kind of a geek before."

"You weren't a geek," he said. "Academic, yes. But not a geek."

"You're my dad," she reminded him. "You have to say that."

"Yes, but I don't think—"

"It's okay, Dad." She sighed loudly. "I know what I was. And I know I don't want to keep on being that. But just because Kate helped me with the outside package doesn't mean my troubles are over."

He frowned. "So you really think that just by reading those"—he nodded to the pile of glossy magazines piled around her feet—"you're going to learn some secret social code for being accepted into a new school?"

"I honestly don't know. Probably not."

"Even if you weren't admitted into whatever high-ranking clique is ruling and reigning in your new school, would it matter so much?"

She laughed. "Oh, Dad, I don't expect to be admitted into any high-ranking clique. Just because my hair is blonde doesn't mean I've lost some brain cells."

He laughed.

"I just want to have something of a life. I don't have high expectations. I just want some good friends and to do some fun things, and not to feel like I need to make myself invisible all the time." She almost added that she also wanted to learn how to deal with boys, but she knew that would probably result in some kind of lecture that she wasn't in the mood to hear right now. Besides, Dad was pulling into one of the freeway motels.

"Last stop until San Jose," he said as he pulled up to the lobby entrance. "I'll be right back."

She could see from where the car was parked that this hotel had a nice-looking outdoor pool, and it looked fairly crowded. Not surprising when the car's exterior thermometer indicated it was 98 degrees out there. And it was past six.

"I think I'll check out the pool," she told Dad when he returned with their room keys. "If you don't mind."

"Not at all. I'll give Kate a call while you're swimming. The hotel restaurant didn't look too bad. Maybe we can just eat in later tonight."

This time as Chelsea got ready to go to the pool, she decided to try out the daring string bikini that Kate had gotten for her. After all, if Kate thought it was okay, why wouldn't it be? Besides, Chelsea figured this would be a good test of whether or not she could act comfortable in her own skin. Of course, once she had the bikini on and saw herself in the bathroom mirror, she nearly fell over at how much of her own skin was actually showing. Even her underwear offered more coverage than this little number. But her faux tan was still holding up, and really, she looked pretty hot in a bikini.

However, she knew her dad might have a stroke if he saw her so scantily clad. Did she want to get him all worked up? She started to switch the bikini for the more conservative suit, then stopped herself. No, she needed to do this. Walking around in public in this bikini would be like her badge of courage. In fact, that's about how big the pieces of the bikini were—like badges.

To bolster her confidence, she touched up her lip gloss and even put on some of the waterproof mascara she'd gotten at their previous hotel gift shop that morning. To protect her dad's heart health, she put her tank top and shorts on over the suit. Grabbing a towel and a few other things, she headed for the door and waved to Dad, who was still on the phone.

"Tell Kate hey for me," she called as she exited. She was relieved he couldn't see her in the bikini. Hopefully he wouldn't venture down to the pool and see his nearly naked daughter.

As she rode the elevator down, she questioned herself. Was she being stupid? Or crazy? Or compromising herself or her values? As the elevator doors opened, she told herself that this was simply going to be a test, and after she passed this test, she would pack the bikini away and never wear it again.

There was an assortment of people in and around the pool. Chelsea found a chair and laid her towel, magazine, and shades on it. Then she slipped off her flip-flops and slowly and carefully peeled off her tank top, making sure that the bikini top stayed in the proper place and that the strings were still securely tied. She slipped off her shorts, also checking the strings on the bikini bottom and wondering if she might be in need of a Brazilian wax job like she'd just read about in one of the magazines. Apparently Brazil was well known for a number of hair-related procedures.

She stood there for a long moment, feeling very conspicuous and uncomfortable and more than a little silly. All her old insecure feelings of extreme shyness, self-consciousness, and fear rushed through her. She wanted to grab her clothes and run and hide. Really, who did she think she was going out in public practically nude? This was something she never would've done before—something she would've made fun of even. What was wrong with her now?

But ignoring these inner voices, she held her head high and slowly walked—make that sauntered—down to the shallow end of the pool. As she did, she felt a number of eyes on her. She feigned oblivion, telling herself she didn't care who stared. Not for the first time, she wished that Virginia and her old "friends" could see her now, but she decided to be content with the eyes that were on her. And there were definitely eyes on her. Eyes of all ages and sorts, but primarily male.

She slowly got into the water and just stood there at waist depth. Then slowly she immersed herself. After the warmth of the air, the water felt cool but not cold. She felt greatly relieved to be concealed, at least partially, by the water. She began to slowly swim, and as she did so she smiled, not particularly because she felt like smiling, but because she hoped it would make her feel more relaxed and at ease.

Finally Chelsea was tired of swimming and even a little weary of her self-imposed test. She felt she had passed, or nearly. She still needed to emerge from the pool, hopefully with the bikini remaining in place. She stood in the shallow end again, taking her time to make adjustments, ensuring that both portions of the bikini were covering what little they covered. She realized that wearing a bikini was no small feat—and in all honestly not as much fun as a suit that covered her better and allowed her to move with more freedom and less self-consciousness. But then, this was a test.

Adopting what she hoped was an air of nonchalance, she slowly went up the steps and out of the pool. She shook her wet hair, and holding her head high, she walked over to her chair. After a bit of towel-drying, which was almost unnecessary in the desert heat, she sat down in the chair, put her shades back on, picked up her magazine, and pretended to be reading. But in actuality she was congratulating herself not only for passing her test but for giving a great performance. With the acting skills she was developing, perhaps she could participate in drama and do more than just paint scenery or help with lighting.

"Hey." A tanned, well-built guy with sandy hair stood over her, looking down with more than a little appreciation. "This seat taken?"

"No." She smiled casually.

"I'm Trey," he said as he moved the chair closer to her and sat down. He looked directly at her with surprising intensity. "You are beautiful."

She laughed. "Well, thanks . . . I guess."

He leaned forward even closer now. His blue eyes sparkled like the pool water, and she could tell by his abs that he worked out regularly and definitely felt comfortable in his own skin. "I mean it. I saw you getting out of the pool just now, and I couldn't believe my eyes. You are really beautiful."

She felt that old familiar warmth rushing up her neck, but she was not going to give in to it. This was just part of her test, and she was determined to ace it. "Well, thanks." She gave him a cheesy smile. "You're sweet."

"I assume you don't live around here, but I'm curious where you're from. And since I told you my name, how about if you tell me yours?"

Trying to maintain the appearance of calmness and confidence and reminding herself of Kate's rules, she told him her name and explained why she and her dad were headed to San Jose. Trey told her that he was from Fort Worth, that he'd come out here with a friend, and that they were checking out a couple of campuses in the area.

"How about spending some time together?" he said. "My bud Craig and I were going to send out for pizzas and order up some pay-per-view flicks. We've got some brewskies already chilling in the fridge. It'd be fun to get to know you better, Chelsea."

Chelsea tried not to appear shocked, but this was all very new to her. She had never been propositioned before. At least that's what she assumed this was. Not that she planned to ask for any specific clarification. But even as a multitude of frantic thoughts ran through her head, she managed to keep a calm smile on her lips. This was her big chance to stay cool in the midst of fire.

"No thanks," she told him. "But I appreciate the offer." Another smile. Not too big, just enough to ooze confidence. She flipped a page of her magazine, like she was done with him.

"Oh, come on," he urged. "We can play some cards or just hang . . . get to know each other. If you want, I can send Craig packing." He grinned like she would appreciate that.

She looked back at him now, tipping her shades up to make direct eye contact. "Really, Trey, I already have dinner plans. But thanks anyway."

This guy was stubborn. He pleaded and begged and cajoled. But she kept her wits about her and never let on how nervous and jittery he was making her feel. She kept reminding herself that this was part of the test. It occurred to her that, for all she knew, he could actually be a sociopathic serial killer. Like that guy with the Dutch name who'd finally been caught in South America.

Finally, growing weary of the game and of Trey, not to mention a little worried, she stood up and told him she needed to go. Of course, this brought a bit of a dilemma. How did she gracefully get back into her shorts and top with him standing there gawking at her? And that was just what he was doing too. Gawking. Plus he just wasn't giving up.

As she slowly gathered her things, he was saying things like "what about after dinner?" and "the night is young," and "who knows when we'll meet again?" like he thought he was starring in some low-budget indie film. She decided to skip trying to redress and simply wrap her towel around her again like a sarong skirt. But as she was tucking it under, Trey placed one hand on her arm—uncomfortably close to her breast, she thought—then leaned forward and touched her cheek with his other hand. "Really, Chelsea, you are the most beautiful creature I've ever laid eyes on, and I can't believe you're ditching me like this. Won't you reconsider?"

"*Excuse* me." Her dad stepped up with a very disturbed expression.

"Hi, Dad," she said nervously.

Trey's hands fell to his side, and as he stepped back with a guilty look, Chelsea felt certain she could see the color draining from his tanned face. In the same instant, she felt the blood rushing to her own.

seven

Chelsea smiled nervously, clutching her things toward her like a shield. "I was just telling Trey that it was time for me to go have dinner with my dad," she said evenly.

"Were you now?" Dad peered at Trey, then at her, and finally back at Trey again.

"That's right." Trey took another step back, almost as if he thought Dad was about to deck him. "She was just leaving."

Dad seemed to see Chelsea's bikini top for the first time, and his reaction looked like a combination of horror and outrage.

"Let's go, Dad." She tugged on his arm. "I'm starving now."

"Yeah, all right." He tossed one last glance at Trey, who was now scurrying away like he couldn't disappear quickly enough.

Before they reached the lobby, she managed to slip her tank top over her head and was just pulling it down to meet the waist of her towel sarong as they reached the elevators.

"Is that one of the, uh, swimsuits Kate got for you?" he asked as they went into the elevator.

She nodded and pushed the button for their floor.

"Well then, I better have myself a talk with that woman."

"Oh, Dad," Chelsea said in a scolding tone. "Don't start calling Kate *that woman*."

"I just want to know where she gets off giving you something like that, Chelsea." His face was getting red, and it looked like he was more than just mildly irritated. Her earlier imaginings of a stroke didn't seem too far-fetched. "It was one thing for Kate to do all this makeover business with you. But if she thinks she can turn you into a little—" He stopped himself, but Chelsea knew by his expression that he'd been about to use an offensive word.

"Dad!" She shook her head like she was disappointed.

"Well, I have a right to my opinion, Chelsea. I am your father." The doors opened to their floor, and Chelsea hurried out ahead. Her dad came sputtering behind her. "You listen to me, Chelsea. Just because you look like a grown-up woman doesn't mean that you are one. You're only sixteen, and you're acting like—"

"I *know* how old I am," she said in a stern but even voice, sticking her key card in the door. "But thanks for reminding me."

"We're going to talk some more about this," he said as she headed straight for the bathroom. "At dinner!"

"Great," she called back as she closed the door. "I can't wait."

She felt a flurry of emotions as she showered. On the one hand, she'd been somewhat relieved to see her dad down by the pool. That whole scene with Trey had been getting weirder and weirder. Yet she'd felt flattered at the attention Trey had been showering on her, and knowing that he was older was kind of cool too. Yet there was that whole sociopath fear. What was up with that?

Now her dad was not only mad at her but at Kate as well. Somehow she needed to smooth this whole thing over. To do that, she decided it would be wise to just tell the truth. Well, most of the truth. She didn't have to tell him everything.

During dinner she explained about wanting to give herself a test. "I wanted to see if I could be comfortable in my own skin," she told him. "And for some reason that bikini seemed like a good idea."

He groaned.

"But I realized that I'm not really comfortable in a swimsuit as skimpy as that."

"Really?" He looked up from his salad with a hopeful expression.

"Yes. I doubt I'll ever wear it again."

He shook his head with a puzzled look. "I just don't know why Kate thought that was appropriate for you."

"Because lots of girls wear bikinis, Dad."

"But that doesn't mean you have to wear something like that."

"I'll bet Kate has a bikini." She shook her finger at him. "And I'll bet that if she wore a bikini on your honeymoon, you wouldn't complain."

He looked embarrassed.

"Would you?"

"I don't know." He shrugged. "I might complain if I saw some guy ogling Kate the way that big testosterone-driven goon was ogling you down by the pool."

Chelsea laughed. "Well, don't worry, Dad. I was actually trying to lose that big testosterone-driven goon anyway."

"That's reassuring." He gave her a relieved smile.

For a moment she considered confessing her crazy fear about how Trey might've been a sociopathic serial killer. But she knew that was ridiculous, and it would probably upset her dad as well. Better to just let this pass and forget about it. In the future, she'd be more careful.

"I'm so glad you're still a sensible girl, Chelsea." Dad took a sip of iced tea. "Even if you look, well, different on the outside, it's good to know you're still the same underneath."

Although she nodded, Chelsea knew that wasn't really true. She wasn't the same underneath anymore. Oh, some things were the same, but she was working hard to change herself. She was determined to evolve far beyond the scared wallflower from before.

As planned, they got up early the next morning. After a long day, in which they took turns driving and practiced the lyrics of the San Jose song, they arrived at the hotel just a little before midnight.

"I got the suite for a full week," Dad told her as they carried their bags down the hallway.

"A suite?" she asked.

"Yes. One side has a kitchen and living room with a pullout bed. There's an adjoining bedroom as well. That way we'll have some space."

"Shall we flip a coin for the bedroom?"

He chuckled. "That's an idea, but I thought I'd let you have it. You've been a real trouper these past few days, but I hear that teen girls need their privacy."

She grinned. "Thanks, Dad."

They both slept in late the next morning, ordering room service around noon and just taking it easy. Then they spent the afternoon driving around and checking out the lay of the land. Dad had already narrowed down which part of the city they'd relocate to, close to the corporate headquarters where he'd be working. After driving by there, he swung by the high school. "Thought you'd like a sneak peek at your new stomping grounds," he told her.

"It looks like a nice school," she said.

"It's ranked quite high in the state," he said. "You might want to check out the school's website and see if you can preregister."

He drove through some of the nearby neighborhoods. It didn't take long before they both agreed that San Sebastian Estates was by far the nicest development, and there were several houses for sale.

"I'm guessing the homes in here will be in the top of our price range," Dad said a bit dismally.

"They say you get what you pay for, Dad."

He chuckled. "Unless you're in the designer discount outlet business. In that case, you get a bargain."

"Oh, Dad." She pointed across the street. "Hey, check out that house—it's for sale."

He parked on the street in front of a pale yellow stucco house and nodded. "That's definitely a nice-looking one."

Chelsea hopped out of the car, grabbed one of the flyers, and started reading. "It's got four bedrooms," she said as she got back in. "And three baths—that would be one for each of us!"

"That sounds good." He leaned over to see the flyer. "The price isn't as bad as I'd expected. It's still a little high, though."

"But you can offer less," she told him. "People do that all the time."

He nodded. "That's true."

"Oh, it has a pool!"

As she continued to gush about the house, Dad agreed to call his Realtor, but all he could do was leave a message. As they drove back to the hotel, Chelsea informed him she wanted to continue being involved in the house hunting. "For Kate's sake," she assured him. "No offense, but I think I might know her tastes better than you."

The next morning the Realtor picked them up at the hotel, and they started looking at properties in San Sebastian. For some reason the Realtor was unenthused about the yellow stucco house. Although he was polite to Chelsea, she could tell he wasn't interested in her opinions when it came to real estate. Finally she pulled Dad into a laundry room of another ho-hum house and closed the door. "Have you noticed that Greg is only showing us houses that are listed with his real estate company?" she said in a hushed tone.

Dad's brow creased. "Now that you mention it . . ."

"And he doesn't want us to look at the yellow stucco house."

"So it seems."

"I think we should lose this Realtor, Dad."

"Maybe so. But first let me give him one more chance to show us the yellow house."

She agreed and they went back out. Greg was looking all pleased with himself now, like he thought they really liked this house and were discussing making an offer on it.

Dad cleared his throat. "Chelsea and I would really like to see that yellow stucco house over on Laredo Lane."

"Oh, you don't want that house," Greg said quickly. "I heard it's had water damage and—"

"I think I need to go back to the hotel." Chelsea held her stomach like she was in pain. "I don't feel too well, Dad."

Dad looked curiously at her, then realizing what she was up to, he played along, even putting his hand on her forehead. "You feel like you might have a fever."

"Uh-huh." She gave a sickly sigh. "Please, Dad, I need to go back to the hotel *now*."

Realtor Greg looked slightly irritated, but he complied, and as soon as they got back to their hotel, Chelsea called the phone number from the flyer for the yellow stucco house, telling the Realtor that they'd meet her there.

"Wow." Dad looked impressed. "Maybe I should let you handle the whole house-buying business."

"Fine with me. Do you want me to drive too?"

"No thanks. Not this time."

Before long they were strolling through the yellow stucco house, which was as sweet inside as out. "Did this house have water damage?" Chelsea asked the Realtor as they stood in the spacious kitchen.

Maria frowned. "Water damage?"

"Another Realtor mentioned something about it."

Maria shook her head. "I've never heard of such a thing here. I haven't seen any repairs or stains to imply that's true. But I can check the insurance records to see."

While Dad asked her more questions, grilling her about utilities and taxes and other boring stuff, Chelsea took another walk through the house. The wood floors echoed as she walked, and she tried to imagine where they'd place their furniture. She decided to call Kate.

"Oh, I'm so glad you answered," Chelsea exclaimed when Kate picked up. "I thought I'd get your voice mail."

"What's up?"

Chelsea told her about the house. "It's so beautiful," she gushed. "I think you'll like it. And there's a pool and a hot tub."

Kate let out a happy squeal. "I like it already!"

Chelsea realized how much she missed Kate. It was like Kate had become her best friend. "I wish you could come out sooner," she said.

"Me too. But I have to honor my commitments here."

"I know." They talked a bit longer, and Chelsea told Kate they'd send some photos of the house. After she hung up, she went back upstairs to look around. She'd already decided that if they got this house, she'd take the bedroom up here. It had a tiny terrace that overlooked the pool, and the bathroom was just across the hall. Besides, she knew Dad and Kate would want the master suite downstairs anyway. It opened right out to the pool.

By the time they left, Dad was as interested in the house as Chelsea. "I'll send Kate the website domain. Maria said it's got some great photos," he said as he drove them back to the hotel. "And she mentioned there's someone else interested in the house—"

"Oh no!"

"She also said it's not too late to make an offer."

"We *have* to make an offer," Chelsea insisted.

By that evening, Kate had seen the website photos and sounded thrilled with the house. The next morning, Dad met with Maria and made an offer. Chelsea hadn't been much of a praying girl, not since middle school when she used to go regularly to youth group with Virginia and her friends, but she actually shot up a little "please, God" offering and hoped that would be better than just crossing her fingers.

There was some back-and-forth negotiating and adjusting on Dad's offer for the house, but three days later Maria called and informed Dad that his offer had been accepted. It turned out that because their offer was cash, thanks to the sale of their previous home, the owners were okay with taking less.

Papers were signed, money changed hands, Dad notified the moving company, and one week later they were given possession of the yellow stucco house on Laredo Lane.

Dad grinned as he handed her the key to the front door. "I think I have you to thank for finding this house. Why don't you do the honors?"

Chelsea unlocked the door and walked inside. Everything still looked as light and bright and pretty as before. She was so happy that she shot up another prayer—a thank-you prayer.

eight

Dad started back to work, and Chelsea took on the task of unpacking crates and boxes and getting things put away. It was hard work, but she was rewarded with breaks by the pool.

"Hello there."

Chelsea jumped and looked up from where she'd been sunning herself to see a girl peering over the stucco wall on the side of the yard. "Uh, hello." She sat up, feeling slightly self-conscious since she had on the barely-there bikini, but she had assumed she'd be safe in her own backyard.

"I'm Janelle Parker," the girl called out. "Sorry to bug you, but I wanted to say hey. I live here, next door."

"Oh." Chelsea tipped up her shades for a better look at the girl in the shadows. "I'm Chelsea Martin."

"So did you guys buy the Ruiz place?"

Chelsea thought for a moment before she remembered the name Ruiz. "Oh, yeah. We did buy it from them. We moved in a few days ago."

"I must've missed that," Janelle said. "I just got back from a summer camp up in Oregon."

"Oh." Chelsea was trying to guess Janelle's age. She seemed young. Twelve, maybe?

"So are you still in school?" Janelle asked. "Or have you graduated already?"

"I'll be a junior in high school."

"Hey, so will I," Janelle said brightly.

"Really?" Chelsea stood and walked over to get a better look at this outgoing girl. For some reason she'd assumed she was younger.

Janelle nodded. "So will you be going to Kingston High?"

"Yeah. My dad drove me by there a few days ago. It seemed nice. Do you like it?"

"Yeah. It's okay."

Chelsea climbed onto a large landscaping rock next to the wall so she could look directly at Janelle. With blue-green eyes, creamy skin, and shiny, shoulder-length brown hair, Janelle was pretty. Not flashy pretty, but pretty in a quieter way. Chelsea glanced past Janelle into her backyard, which was mostly grass. "You guys don't have a pool too?"

Janelle made a face. "My dad hates pools. He says they're a hole in the ground you throw money into."

Chelsea nodded. "My dad wasn't totally excited about a pool either, but I promised to help with the maintenance. Now I just need to learn how to do that."

"I can help if you want."

"I thought you said your dad hated—"

"The house before this one had a pool. He hated it. That's why we moved."

"Oh."

Janelle sighed. "I still miss it. Especially on hot days like today."

"Do you want to come over?"

Janelle brightened. "Sure. I mean, if you really want me to. I hope I didn't sound like I was hinting for an invite."

Chelsea laughed. "No, not at all. The truth is it's been kind of lonely. It would be nice to get to know someone."

Janelle looked curiously at Chelsea. "It must've been hard for you to leave all your friends behind. Were you really bummed to move?"

"Yeah, it was hard to move. But the truth is I didn't have that many friends." As soon as those words were out, Chelsea wished she'd been more cautious.

Janelle looked surprised and even a little dubious. "Really? Why is that?"

"It's a long story," Chelsea said.

"Okay then, if you really don't mind me crashing in on you, I'll go change into my suit and come over, and maybe you'll tell me your long story."

Chelsea nodded and climbed down from the stone, but as Janelle disappeared back behind the wall, Chelsea wondered how much she really wanted to tell this girl. She didn't even know her. How much could she trust her? Especially since they'd be going to the same school in a few weeks. Chelsea remembered how Virginia and the others had hurt her. Did she want to go through that again?

By the time Janelle rang the doorbell, Chelsea had decided to play it safe. She would be careful with how much information she disclosed, and at the same time she'd try to figure out what kind of a person Janelle really was. She would start by finding out how much she actually knew about pool maintenance.

To Chelsea's surprise, Janelle not only knew a lot about pools, she was a hard worker and she seemed pretty smart too. And she was funny. By the time they went back into the house to take a break from the sun, Chelsea realized that she actually liked Janelle.

"You still haven't told me why you didn't have many friends at your old school," Janelle said as she peeled newsprint from a glass tumbler and set it on the countertop. She was helping Chelsea to unpack. But because she was short, barely five feet tall, Chelsea was putting things in the upper cabinets.

"I wasn't sure I really wanted to tell you," Chelsea said slowly. She set a stack of plates on a high shelf.

"My mom's always telling me I'm way too nosy." Janelle smiled apologetically. "I guess I'm just overly curious. Sorry."

"No, that's okay." Chelsea decided to just tell her. Janelle seemed trustworthy. Really, what did Chelsea have to be afraid of? So she spilled the beans, telling how she'd been an ugly duckling wallflower and how her soon-to-be step-mom had made her over.

"That's hard to believe," Janelle said finally.

"I know." Chelsea went over to the wall mirror that she'd hung in the dining area and looked at herself. Her hair was a little stringy from the pool and her face was devoid of makeup, but even so, she still looked much better than before the makeover. "Trust me, it's hard for me to believe too."

"So what are your interests?" Janelle asked from where she was opening another box in the kitchen.

Chelsea came back and started removing pots and pans from a crate. "Well, the truth is I've always been kind of an academic nerd. I think I replaced friends with books, high grades, and an obsession on education."

"A good education can come in handy."

"I know. But now I want something more too. I feel like I've been socially starved."

Janelle laughed. "Socially starved?"

"Seriously. I've been lonely for years. And since we moved here, I've even been missing my dad's fiancée. How lame is that?"

"Well, Kingston is a big school. You should have your choice of friends."

Chelsea nodded, but she wondered what that meant. Was Janelle gently hinting that she didn't have room in her social life for Chelsea, and that she'd have to find her own friends?

"So you must have some other interests," Janelle persisted. "Beyond academics, I mean."

"Well, I do have this weird addiction to a couple of reality shows." Chelsea felt embarrassed. Maybe she was truly hopeless. All those years of retreating and hiding might have permanently damaged her. Maybe she was socially retarded. But she reminded herself of one of Kate's self-confidence rules. *Keep your inner voice upbeat and positive. Don't listen to the lies.*

"I'm into drama," Janelle told her. "Last year I got to play Puck in *A Midsummer Night's Dream.*"

"I thought Puck was a guy."

"We made him unisex." She laughed, waving her hand over her petite form, which was much less curvy than Chelsea's. "Besides, as you can see, I can still pass for a boy."

"You know, I've been thinking about getting more involved in drama. I was in drama before, but thanks to my social anxieties, I remained way back behind the scenes."

"With your looks, you could probably get a good part. That is, if you can act."

"I'd be willing to try." Chelsea didn't want to admit that she felt like she was acting most of the time these days anyway. Mostly she hoped her act would feel natural by the time school started. She just needed to get some more practice in the meantime.

Janelle tossed an empty box onto a stack of others. "Hey, we're almost done in here."

"Thanks so much for helping."

Janelle looked at the clock on the stove. "I should probably get going. I have a youth group thing at six."

"Youth group?"

Janelle shrugged like she was uncomfortable. "You know, for church."

"Oh."

"Are you into that sort of thing?" Janelle seemed tentative.

Chelsea shrugged. "I don't know."

"I mean, a lot of kids think it's kinda lame to still be going to youth group in high school."

"I don't think it's lame. What kind of church do you belong to anyway?"

"It's a nondenominational Christian church. And the youth group is actually pretty cool. Tonight's a barbecue, and if you want, you'd be more than welcome to come along."

"Really?"

Janelle seemed surprised. "Absolutely. You really want to?"

Chelsea nodded. "Sure."

"Cool. We need to be ready to leave by 5:30 since I'm helping to set up the drinks table. Can you be ready by then?"

"No problem. How do we get there?"

"Alice is picking me up. She's one of the leaders. The barbecue is at a park near the church, and you can dress pretty casual. Just come over to my house when you're ready. Okay?"

"Sounds good."

After Janelle left, Chelsea called Dad to let him know she was going out. At first he sounded concerned, but when she assured him that a youth leader was driving and that Janelle lived right next door, he seemed pleased. "That sounds great," he told her. "In fact, I've been thinking it might be good to get involved in a church again. It's like we sort of lost track of all that when your mom died."

"I know." Chelsea felt sad to remember how she'd gotten uncomfortable being around Virginia and the other girls at church and how she'd let that discourage her from attending. "I guess that was my fault."

"I'm glad to hear you're doing this, Chels. Have fun!"

"Thanks." Chelsea hurried to take a shower, blow her hair dry, and do her makeup. Then she went to her new room, where everything was already unpacked and in its place. She opened her new walk-in closet and looked at the wardrobe Kate had helped her to build and wondered what to wear. Janelle had said casual, but Chelsea didn't want to be too casual. She might be meeting kids she'd go to school with, and she wanted to make a good first impression.

She pulled out several items, holding them up in front of the mirror attached to the back of the closet door. Finally she decided on a white denim skirt. Stitched like jeans, it was kind of like shorts and it showed off her legs. She topped this with a light blue cami top that accentuated her tan as well as her curves. She added sandals and some hoop earrings that Kate said went with everything, then fluffed her hair, retouched her lip gloss, and took one last look in the mirror. She knew she looked hot.

Thinking that this youth group barbecue would be the perfect opportunity to practice her self-confidence tricks, she looped her new canvas Chloe bag over her shoulder and donned her favorite Gucci shades—all purchased at bargain prices. Feeling like a million bucks, she locked the house and headed next door.

"Wow." Janelle looked surprised when she opened the door. "You clean up nicely."

Chelsea laughed. "Well, thanks, I guess."

Janelle introduced Chelsea to her mom as they picked up some grocery bags of drinks. Before they left the kitchen, a dark-haired guy came in, and Janelle introduced him as her older brother Grayson. "He just graduated high school last year."

"Nice to meet you." Grayson's eyes lit up as he shook her hand.

"Chelsea's the same age as me," Janelle told him. "She and her dad just moved into the Ruiz house."

He made a disappointed face. "Too bad you didn't move here last year."

"Why?" Chelsea asked.

He smiled. "Then we would've been in school together."

Janelle gave him a sisterly punch in the arm. "Grayson's getting ready to go to school back east. He leaves next week."

"I think your ride's here," her mom called from another room.

"A real pleasure to meet you, Chelsea," Grayson said.

"You know, you could always come to youth group tonight if you want to," Janelle called after him.

Grayson looked at Chelsea again. "That's tempting." He shook his head. "Except that's for high school kids."

"Yes, and you're so beyond that now." Janelle laughed as they went out the front door to where a small car was waiting in the driveway. "Brothers!"

They put the bags in the trunk, and as they got into the backseat, Janelle introduced Chelsea to Alice, one of the youth leaders, and a girl named Bretta, who was sitting on the passenger side. Janelle quickly filled Bretta and Alice in on Chelsea. "Bretta's a senior at Kingston," she added.

The three girls made small talk as Alice drove. Chelsea tried to insert a comment here and there, but as she looked around the car, she realized that she was actually overdressed. Everyone else had on shorts and T-shirts. Still, Chelsea decided, she would not let this get to her. In some ways, it was no different than being in a bikini. She just needed to remember Kate's rules for confidence. It would be good practice. And judging by the butterflies in her stomach just now, she still needed the practice.

nine

At the park, Chelsea helped Janelle set up the drinks table by opening cases of soda and bags of ice and arranging them in a cooler. It didn't take long, and then a game of volleyball was organized.

"Want to play?" Janelle asked.

Chelsea considered her white skirt and cami top and how they might fare on a volleyball court, then shook her head. "I'm not really that good at volleyball," she admitted, which was true. "Maybe I'll just cheer from the sidelines."

"Okay." Janelle nodded, then ran over to the sandy area where the nets were set up.

Chelsea found a nearby bench, and feeling slightly out of place but determined not to show it, she sat down. She crossed one leg over the other and pretended to be comfortable, watching the volleyball players jumping and leaping and yelling as the game heated up. They seemed to be having fun, and part of her was frustrated at not being able to participate, but another part was relieved. *Pacing is everything*, she thought. *Give yourself time.*

"Are you part of this group?"

Chelsea looked up to see a lanky blond guy looking down at her with a semi-serious expression. He had on khaki shorts, a sports T-shirt, and a ball cap. "What do you mean?" she asked.

He sat down next to her. "The youth group. I mean, I haven't seen you around before, have I?"

"Oh, well, no." She explained about being new in town and her recent connection to Janelle.

"That's cool." He smiled. "Very cool. I'm Chase Lassiter. My dad's actually one of the pastors at church, so I guess I can officially welcome you to our youth group."

"So when your dad's a pastor, does that mean you're forced to participate in youth group?"

He laughed. "Not exactly, but that's not far from the truth either."

"I wasn't suggesting that it's not cool or anything." She adjusted her shades. "I mean, this is my first visit. It looks like people are having a good time."

He tipped his head toward the volleyball area. "So you're not the athletic type then?"

She shrugged. "Not so much today."

"In that case, I'm not either." He began questioning her about where she was from and what grade she was in and all the usual stuff. She could tell that he was more than a little interested in her.

Another guy came over to them. Like Chase, he was tall, but his hair was dark and wavy. In Chelsea's opinion, he was better looking. "Hey, Lassiter, what are you doing over here warming the bench instead of playing?"

"This is Nicholas Prague," Chase told her. "He can be a real pest, but we put up with him." He introduced Chelsea, explaining that she was new in town.

"Welcome." Nicholas seemed to study her, not in the way Chase had, but as if he was curious about her. "So I take it you're not into volleyball?"

"Not today she's not," Chase answered for her.

"I'd rather just watch," she said.

Nicholas nodded. "That's understandable." He turned to Chase. "What's your excuse?"

"I'm keeping Chelsea company." Chase gave a cheesy smile. "We want to make newcomers welcome, right?"

Nicholas looked dubious. "Well, it's nice to meet you, Chelsea—and I do hope you feel welcome." He pointed at Chase. "But watch out for that one."

Chase just laughed. Nicholas jogged over to join in the reorganizing of the next volleyball game, inserting himself right in the middle of the action.

Janelle came back. "Hey, I see you've met trouble." She sat down next to Chase, jabbing him with her elbow. "Why aren't you out there playing?"

"Why aren't you?" he retorted.

"Didn't you see me out there busting some moves?" She acted offended. "Excuse me for taking a break, but it's like a hundred degrees in the sun." She fanned herself with her hand.

He chuckled. "Why don't you go get yourself something to drink?"

"Why don't you go get me something?" she shot back at him.

"Okay, okay." He held up his hand and stood. He looked

at Chelsea. "How about you? Can I bring you back a soda too?"

They told him what they wanted, then while he was gone, Janelle asked Chelsea what she thought of Chase.

"He seems nice enough."

"Just nice?" Janelle questioned.

Chelsea shrugged. "I guess."

"Because I'll warn you," Janelle said quietly. "Chase and I have been involved in an on-again, off-again relationship for more than a year now."

"Oh . . . right." Chelsea slowly nodded. "I get it. So what are you now? On again or off again?"

Janelle frowned. "Off again . . . unfortunately."

"I see." Chelsea looked up to see Chase coming back.

"Don't let on that I told you anything, okay?"

"Sure. No problem." Chelsea glanced over to the volley-ball match. Nicholas reached down to help a guy back up to his feet and slapped him on the back with a warm smile. For some reason it was Nicholas Prague who interested her most. Even his name was interesting.

"I noticed you met Nicholas too," Janelle said.

"Uh-huh."

"He's really a good guy."

"Who's a good guy?" Chase asked as he presented them with their sodas. "Are you talking about me again, Janelle, darling?" He winked at Chelsea. "You know, Janelle is president of the Chase Lassiter Fan Club."

"You are seriously disturbed, Chase." Janelle made a face at him. "Not to mention totally narcissistic."

"But you still like me, don't you?" he teased.

"And did I say delusional?" She took a sip of her soda,

then wiped the cool can across her forehead. "I'd rather go out there and bake my brain in the sun than listen to your self-absorbed egotistical blather."

He laughed loudly. "Self-absorbed egotistical blather? Really, Janelle, is that any way to talk to your brother in Christ?"

She rolled her eyes and stood. "It was better than resorting to foul language."

Chelsea giggled.

"You sure you don't want to come out and play with us?" Janelle smiled appealingly. "Get away from this conceited jerk?"

"Thanks, but I'm not into baking my brain today."

"Besides, I plan to talk Chelsea into helping me with the grilling." Chase smiled. "I'm the head burger chef tonight, and I really could use an assistant. You interested?"

"Sure," she said, then looked at Janelle with uncertainty. "I mean, unless Janelle wants to help," she added quickly.

Janelle waved her hand. "No way. You go ahead. It's probably hotter by the grills than the volleyball court anyway."

They parted ways, and soon Chelsea, garbed in an apron, was flipping burgers and squirting sauce and trying to keep the barbecue from turning into an inferno. As she worked to keep the burgers from becoming burnt offerings, she wondered whether she was assisting Chase or doing all the work herself. What had become of the head burger chef? She was flipping the burgers for the second time when she felt someone massaging her shoulders.

"Great work," Chase said. "Keep it up, champ."

"Hey, aren't you supposed to be doing this?"

"Yeah, but I had to go help with the condiments."

"Oh, sure," she joked, "leave me over in the hot spot while you slice tomatoes."

"I didn't get to be head chef for nothing." He continued to rub her shoulders like he was enjoying it more than she was. "But if you work hard enough, I might promote you from grill patrol to pickles."

She laughed and turned around, noticing that Janelle was watching her from the table area. "Here," she said, handing him the burger flipper. "I'm taking a break." She removed her apron and handed it to him as well, then she walked over to where Janelle was opening a package of paper plates. "Your Chase is quite a character."

"*My* Chase?" Janelle looked skeptical.

"Well, he's more yours than mine." Chelsea picked up a package of napkins and started to open them.

"Don't be so sure."

More kids were coming to the table now, and it was clear that everyone was getting hungry. Janelle introduced Chelsea to lots of them, but the names were getting jumbled in her head. So she just smiled, made eye contact, and acted like she was perfectly at ease with the group. She was surprised at how friendly everyone seemed, like she was an old friend.

As the evening progressed, first with food—which was followed by some hilarious icebreaker games—and then with dessert, she couldn't help but notice that the guys in this group were even friendlier than the girls. With the exception of one guy. Unfortunately, it was the only guy that Chelsea felt interested in. For some reason Nicholas Prague was acting chilly toward her. It was as if he wanted to keep her at a distance. For some reason she found this rather unsettling.

Eventually the youth leader, Raymond, picked up a guitar and called everyone over to a grassy area. "We don't have the band all set up tonight, but I thought I'd lead us in some worship songs." He started playing, and everyone started singing along—they knew the words—and the whole mood of the group got a little more serious, or perhaps focused. Chelsea was standing with Janelle and Bretta. She knew that Chase was behind her, but she couldn't see where Nicholas was, and even though she told herself not to, she was looking around, hoping to spot him.

After the singing portion ended, Raymond invited everyone to sit down on the grass and then said a prayer. After that he began to introduce someone who was going to speak. Judging by Raymond's words, this person was pretty special.

"I've known this guy for years, and I've watched him go through some struggles, some losses, some changes . . . but I've also watched him growing in the Lord—more so than ever during the past year. So why don't you all give it up for your buddy and mine, Nicholas Prague."

Chelsea was surprised to see Nicholas step forward. She was equally surprised to realize that somehow, as they'd rearranged themselves to sit down on the grass, Chase had managed to squeeze in between her and Janelle. Of course, this should please Janelle . . . sort of. But Chelsea felt uncomfortable with how close Chase was sitting next to her, like he was leaning into her on purpose. And every time she glanced his way, he seemed to be fixated on her. Seriously, it was like he had stars in his eyes.

For sanity's sake, she decided to ignore him, locking her gaze on Nicholas. She wanted to figure this guy out. For some reason she'd assumed he was her age or thereabouts. But here he was up in front, speaking to the youth group—and doing it as if it came easily to him. Did that mean he was one of the youth leaders, or was he already in college, or what?

Nicholas was telling them about his family history. Although his parents had always been a churchgoing family, they'd suddenly gotten divorced when he was fourteen. He told about how hard it was for him to learn that his dad had been involved in an affair, and how it had really unraveled his life when his dad seemed to abandon his family. Nicholas talked about going through some rebellious times for a couple of years. It sounded like he'd broken all the rules. Then he talked about how the youth pastor, Raymond, had befriended him, spending time with him. And how he had recommitted his life to God.

"I'm not saying that it's all been easy since then," Nicholas said. "I'm just saying that when I finally reached the end of myself and I accepted my need for God, it did get better. It was like the clouds cleared away. I started to feel hopeful about the future. A lot of you guys know about how I've had my ups and downs. But thanks to a relationship with God, my ups are becoming more regular, and when I'm down I know that God is ready to lift me up."

Finally he talked about recently working at a summer youth camp for kids from divorced families. "Helping these kids for the past six weeks was so awesome," he said, his blue eyes sparkling. "I didn't realize that I had so much to give. It was like all the pain and crud I'd gone through the past few years was suddenly useful because I could relate to these kids. I could tell them I knew what it felt like. There's a Scripture that says everything works together for good if you love God. It's like that became reality to me. I could see how God took something totally miserable and turned it into something precious. It was amazing."

He talked a bit more, but Chelsea was so touched that she actually felt on the verge of tears. She'd never known a guy like this. So sincere. So sold-out for God. It was mind-boggling. She really wanted to hear more.

But afterward, Nicholas was flocked by a small crowd of kids asking him questions or slapping him on the back. Although Chelsea wanted to talk to him, to ask him questions of her own, she held back.

"So, Chelsea," Chase said. He slipped an arm around her shoulders in what she assumed was meant to look like a "brotherly" way but felt like more. "What do you think of our little old youth group? Not as stodgy as you thought we'd be?"

"I think you guys are pretty cool." She tried to step away, but he just moved along with her. Janelle was over talking to some other kids, and suddenly Chelsea felt kind of trapped.

"There's going to be a really cool Christian rock concert over in Palo Alto next Saturday. Do you think you'd want to go?"

"I, uh, I don't know." She didn't like this feeling, like she wasn't in control. But she knew she couldn't let Chase or the situation get the best of her. She reached around, plucked his hand from her shoulder, and turned to look directly at him. "Do you mind if I think about it a little?"

"Not at all."

"I wonder if Janelle would like to go too."

He shrugged. "Maybe so."

"How about getting a bunch of friends together?" she asked. "Then we could all go to the concert together."

He smiled. "Sure, why not."

She glanced over to where Nicholas was still surrounded. "Maybe your buddy Nicholas would want to come too."

"Yeah, I could ask him."

Janelle was coming back over to join them, and Chelsea told her about the plan. "Doesn't that sound like fun?"

Janelle looked somewhat surprised. "Sure, I guess so."

"Okay." Chelsea nodded. "If Janelle is in, I am too."

"Great. I'll give you girls a call with the details."

"Why don't you call Janelle," Chelsea suggested, "and she can let me know."

Chase cocked his head to one side. "Are you afraid to give out your phone number?"

"No. I just need to change to a cheaper cellular provider, and we don't have a landline yet."

He nodded. "Oh, yeah, that makes sense."

"I assume you know Janelle's number." Chelsea gave Janelle a sly glance.

"If he can remember that far back," Janelle teased. She tipped her head over to where Alice and Bretta were standing. "I think Alice wants to get going. She needs to get home before too late since she has to work in the morning."

"Well, let's not be strangers," Chase said to Chelsea.

Chelsea smiled. "See ya around."

As they rode home, Chelsea was still thinking about Nicholas. She wished she'd had the nerve to go up and talk to him. Hopefully he'd agree to go to the concert with them on Saturday. Too bad she hadn't told Chase that she wouldn't go unless Nicholas went. Of course, that might've seemed a little odd.

"I really liked hearing that guy speak tonight," Chelsea said when there was a lull in the conversation.

"You mean Nicholas?" Alice said.

"Yeah. What he said was interesting . . . but somehow I'd gotten the impression he was still in high school."

"He is still in high school," Bretta said. "He's a senior this year."

"Oh?" Chelsea nodded. "He seems mature for a senior."

Bretta laughed. "That's probably because you're a junior."

Chelsea and Janelle exchanged glances, then giggled.

"I've known Nicholas since we were little kids," Bretta said. "Our parents are friends."

"So he goes to Kingston High too?" Chelsea hoped she didn't sound too curious.

"Yeah. Most of the youth group kids go there."

Chelsea felt a wave of relief. Maybe she'd get a chance to know Nicholas better after all. Hopefully he'd want to get to know her too.

ten

t wasn't until the following afternoon that Chelsea began to wonder if she'd done something to offend Janelle. She'd called her cell phone a couple of times, inviting her to come over to use the pool and hang out again. But Janelle's initial response was vague, and on the second call she was actually chilly.

As Chelsea was putting books on a bookshelf, she started to flash back to the time when Virginia had grown cold and distant and their friendship had quickly disintegrated. Was it possible that was happening again? Not that Chelsea had entertained any illusions that Janelle would become her instant best friend. But she thought they'd had fun yesterday, and she really did like Janelle.

Taking a break by the pool, Chelsea was absorbed in a book when she heard someone calling to her over Janelle's side of the wall. To her surprise, Chase Lassiter was waving at her. "Hey, Chelsea, what's up?"

Wishing she'd put on the swimsuit with more coverage, she waved meekly and grabbed her towel. "Not much. Where's Janelle?"

"In the house."

"Oh." Chelsea nodded. Naturally, she was wondering what Chase was doing. If he was visiting Janelle, why was he gawking at Chelsea over the stucco wall?

"Want any company over there?" He grinned.

Chelsea stood, wrapping her large beach towel around her like a sarong dress. "Well, I invited Janelle over, but she didn't seem too interested."

"I didn't mean Janelle."

"Maybe you didn't, but I did." Chelsea secured the top of her towel. "I'd like to talk to her."

"Want me to get her?" he offered.

"Sure." Chelsea felt uneasy as she watched him disappear from the wall. Was it possible that the problem with Janelle was related to Chase? If so, how could Chelsea assure Janelle that she had absolutely no interest in him? She thought hard as she waited, trying to construct some kind of plan or strategy in her head.

"Chase said you want to talk to me." Janelle's head was now visible above the wall.

Chelsea slipped on her flip-flops and walked over to climb onto the rock. "I wondered if I did something to offend you," she began. "If so, I'm sorry."

Janelle's lips were pressed tightly together.

"Chase was kind of inviting himself over here," Chelsea continued. "But I hinted to him that I'd prefer your company to his."

Janelle looked surprised. "Seriously?"

Chelsea nodded. "I'm not into Chase, Janelle. Not even a little."

"Really?" Janelle still looked skeptical.

"I swear I'm not."

"Maybe you should tell him that."

"Hey, I'd be happy to."

Janelle's brows arched. "Fine. I'll go get him."

"Why don't you guys come over here," Chelsea suggested. "Might be easier than hanging over this wall."

A few minutes later, the three of them were sitting in the family room at Chelsea's.

"Go ahead," Janelle told Chelsea. "Tell him."

"Tell me what?" Chase looked hopeful.

"I'm not sure you care," Chelsea began uncertainly, "but in case you had the wrong idea, I was just telling Janelle that I'm not interested in you. I mean, for anything beyond a friend." Now she felt really embarrassed. What if she was making a fool of herself? What if Chase only wanted to be friends too?

"So you don't want to go out with me?" He looked surprised. "What about the concert next weekend?"

"Did you think that was a date?"

"Sure." He nodded.

"Well, I'm sorry if I gave you the wrong impression. I thought it was just going to be friends going out together."

"You're serious?" Chase still looked unconvinced.

"Listen to her," Janelle told him with a hint of impatience. "She's making it pretty clear." She smiled at Chelsea.

"Really, Chase," Chelsea continued. "I'm sorry if I was unclear. To be honest, I haven't, uh, dated much, and this is a little new to me."

He laughed. "Yeah, right. And you'd probably like to sell me a bridge too."

"Huh?" Chelsea didn't know what else to say.

"She's telling the truth," Janelle said quickly.

"Not that I want to go into all that," Chelsea told him. "How about we just leave it at this—I'm not interested in dating you, Chase. You seem like a nice guy. But I'm not into you."

Chase smiled weakly. "Okay, okay . . . I can take a hint."

"I hope we can still be friends." Chelsea smiled back.

Chase brightened. "Sure. In fact, my dad is always saying that all good romantic relationships start with good friendships."

Chelsea exchanged glances with Janelle, then shrugged.

"So what are you girls up to today?" Chase asked.

"I'm still unpacking things." Chelsea pointed over to the partially filled box of books.

"Need some help?"

"No thanks," Chelsea said quickly. "I can handle it."

Chase slowly stood. "Like I said, I can take a hint."

Chelsea smiled. "I appreciate the offer, Chase. It's just that I have to figure out which stuff goes where. I don't really need help. Okay?"

"It's okay." He grinned. "See you girls around then."

Janelle gave a halfhearted finger wave, inviting him to see himself out, and Chelsea merely said, "Bye-bye," and then he was gone.

Chelsea turned to Janelle. "I'm sorry about that. I honestly wasn't trying to start anything with him."

"I know." Janelle sighed. "Chase is just like that. Some people think he's a total jerk. Sometimes I do too. But he was my first boyfriend . . . I guess that makes me a little soft when it comes to him."

Chelsea considered this. "Maybe you're too soft."

Janelle nodded. "Yeah . . . probably."

"So are we still friends?" Chelsea asked.

"Sure." Janelle went over to the box of books. "You really don't want some help with this?"

"Actually, I'd love help. I just didn't want Chase's help."

Janelle laughed. "How about I unpack and hand them to you, and you put them away?"

"Sounds good."

They worked together, and Chelsea could tell they were moving more than twice as fast as Chelsea would have by herself. "My mom used to say that many hands make light work."

"Are your parents divorced?"

Chelsea explained the situation, and Janelle was very sympathetic. "That must've been hard."

Chelsea nodded as she knelt down to fit the last of the books on the bottom shelf. "Yeah. I think losing my mom made it even easier for me to sort of fade into the woodwork at school. It's like I wanted to just stop existing."

Janelle placed a hand on Chelsea's shoulder. "Well, it's definitely time for you to start existing. And I'm sorry I was so jealous of you."

"You were jealous of me?" Chelsea stood and stared at Janelle.

Janelle laughed. "Duh. Wasn't it obvious?"

Chelsea thought about it. "Well, I did wonder. But honestly, this is still new to me. Have you ever heard about amputees who have phantom pain after losing a limb?"

Janelle nodded with a confused expression.

"Sometimes I can relate to that. It's like I still have phantom pain from all those years of feeling like a misfit, and I forget that it's not who I am anymore."

"I get it. Kind of like BDD. I mean body dysmorphic disorder."

"You mean when skinny girls look in the mirror and think they're fat?"

"It's more than just that. I actually did a report on it for health last year. BDD includes all kinds of things. It is about perception—rather, misperception—but someone with BDD can be obsessed about anything from a few zits to some extra weight or a crooked nose. They see these things as far worse than they really are and go to all kinds of extremes, including plastic surgery, to fix them. They don't understand that the problem is in their head, not their body."

Chelsea remembered how she used to obsess over her bad complexion, her lack of breasts, and a multitude of other things. What if she had BDD? "How does a person know that she, uh, has this disorder?"

Janelle looked thoughtful. "Let me see if I can remember the symptoms. Obviously any preoccupation with your looks or thinking that something's wrong with you or that everyone else is prettier. And if you look in the mirror all the time or you're always primping and trying to look perfect. Or avoiding socializing. Why?"

Chelsea frowned. "I just hope I don't have it."

Janelle shook her head. "You seem pretty confident to me. At the barbecue, you were, like, the belle of the ball."

"Really?" Chelsea pushed a strand of hair from her face. "That's not how I felt."

"Well, maybe you're a better actress than you think."

Chelsea chuckled. "Guess I should go out for drama after all."

"For sure. And speaking of school, I wanted to do some back-to-school shopping tomorrow. Are you interested?"

Chelsea shrugged. "I'm not really much of a shopper."

"Really? Well, you could've fooled me by the outfit you had on yesterday. That was pretty hot. And after I told you the barbecue was casual too. I was wondering how you'd look if you were really trying."

Chelsea grinned sheepishly. "My dad's fiancée helped me to shop. She's really good at it. You should see my closet."

"Okay!"

"Seriously? You want to see my closet?"

"Sure."

They trekked upstairs, and Chelsea showed Janelle her room and her closet. "I guess there's still a lot of room in it," she admitted. "But this is the best my closet has ever looked."

"Wow." Janelle walked around, looking at everything. "Your future stepmom really has superb taste. You're lucky, Chelsea."

"Yeah. Kate is pretty cool."

"And you like her?"

"Absolutely. I mean, I didn't at first. But when I got to know her, she was more like a friend than a mom."

"Cool." Janelle took out the Kate Spade purse. "This is awesome. It must've cost a fortune."

Chelsea told her about the designer discount outlet store. "It's called Best 4 Less."

"I've heard of it. Is it any good?"

Chelsea admitted that her dad worked for the company. "I get a nice discount on top of the reduced prices, which means some awesome deals. But if you shop at the right times, like after a new shipment arrives, you can score some cool stuff too." Suddenly she had an idea. "Hey, why don't we go together sometime? I could let you use my discount. I mean, as long as I purchase the item, then you pay me back." Chelsea assumed that since it was okay to do that with Kate, it would be okay to do it with Janelle too, but maybe she would check with her dad to be sure.

"That would be fabulous."

"I'll check to see when the new shipments come in at the local stores."

"Cool." Janelle held up a BCBG top. "Too bad we're not the same size. We could do clothes swapping." She chuckled. "Of course, I don't have nearly as cool of stuff as you do." She tapped a purse. "But then there are the one-size-fits-all items too."

Chelsea was unsure. It had been so long since she'd played the friend game that she didn't quite know what was expected, so she just exited the closet. Grabbing her mom's old guitar, she sat down on the bed and started to pick around on it.

"Wow, you play guitar?" Janelle sat down in the chair across from the bed.

"Not very well. My mom had just started teaching me before she died. I took some lessons for a while, then I started playing on my own. I'm sure someone who really knows how to play would laugh."

"I don't know how to play, but I know what sounds good. Let's hear what you can do."

Chelsea played for a bit, but feeling self-conscious and amateurish, she stopped.

"That seemed pretty good to me," Janelle told her. "My

brother plays, and so do some kids at church. In fact, there's a guitar class that's kind of ongoing. Remember Raymond?"

"The youth pastor?"

"Uh-huh. He teaches it. You might want to check it out."

"Yeah. Maybe so."

After a while they got something to eat, then went to hang by the pool some more. As Chelsea lazily swam some laps, she told herself not to get her hopes up too high, but it did seem like this was the beginning of a genuine friendship. She felt like she'd barely avoided a train wreck with that Chase business earlier. But she'd been honest, and Janelle had seemed okay about it. Hopefully that would be the biggest obstacle between them now.

Chelsea got out of the pool and toweled dry, then after some small talk about shoes, she ran into the house to get them each a fresh soda. As she filled tall glasses with ice, she realized that her social skills were awkward at best. She wanted to give this friendship her best shot, but without making it look like she was putting as much effort as she was into it. More than anything, Chelsea wanted a friend by her side when school started. However, she wasn't sure that Janelle didn't have other friends . . . closer friends. What if there wasn't room for one more? How could Chelsea be sure to carve a solid position into Janelle's social structure?

eleven

Chelsea knew that, despite appearances, Janelle was into fashion. As ironic as it seemed, thanks to Kate, Chelsea suspected she was just a couple steps ahead of Janelle when it came to style. On her way back outside, she grabbed some of the glossy fat fashion magazines, ones she'd gathered on the trip out here. Chelsea's plan was to maintain the pretense that she knew something about clothes and shoes and things in the hopes of solidifying their friendship.

"Here you go." She handed Janelle a glass of soda, then dumped the pile of magazines on the table between the chaise lounges. "You might want to check out what's hot for this fall," she said casually. She stretched out on her own lounge and took a nice cool sip.

"Yoo-hoo!" A strange call seemed to come out of the blue. It was followed by a low whistle.

Chelsea looked up and around the yard. "What was that?"

"I'd say it was Grayson, except it's coming from over there." Janelle pointed to where the row of trees grew along the back stucco wall. She lowered her voice. "And that's where *Hollywood* lives."

"Huh?" Chelsea studied Janelle. "Who is—"

"Dayton Moore," Janelle whispered as she peered across the pool to the back wall. "But I doubt that it's really him. He's such a—"

"Hey, ladies," a guy's voice called out.

"Dayton?" Janelle yelled back.

"You know me?"

Janelle stood up and walked around to the other side of the pool deck where she could see better. Chelsea remained behind just watching to see what transpired.

"Why wouldn't I know you?" Janelle demanded.

"Oh, it's just Baby Face Parker." He sounded disappointed as he hoisted himself to the top of the wall, perching there with one knee under his elbow like he thought he was posing for a photo. "You don't even live here, Baby Face." He pointed at Chelsea. "But tell me, *who* is that?"

"That is my friend," Janelle said in a snooty voice. "And she happens to live here."

"I see." He grinned and waved at Chelsea. "Hello, neighbor!"

"Fine," Janelle said sharply. "You said hello, now leave us alone."

But the guy hopped off the wall and into Chelsea's yard. With a confident stride, he came toward her. Her old instincts told her to get up and run the other way—that this was the kind of guy who ignored girls like her, or worse. But instead of giving in to those old fears, she stayed put. Keeping a blasé expression, she took in a slow, deep breath, and using her hand as a visor for the glare over the top of her shades, she simply looked at him. His short, cropped hair was sandy brown, and he was wearing navy athletic shorts and a sleeveless white T-shirt that showed off some well-developed and tanned biceps. As he got closer, she could see that his features were even and tanned and that he was good-looking. In fact, he was extremely good-looking. Uncomfortably good-looking.

"I just wanted to be neighborly." He gave a mock bow as he looked down at her. "I'm Dayton Moore." He jerked his thumb over his shoulder. "I live back there."

Chelsea sat up and swung her legs around, then stood and extended her hand. "Pleased to meet you, Dayton Moore. I'm Chelsea Martin."

"Pleased to meet *you*." He continued to hold her hand, and despite his sporty shades, she could sense him checking her out—closely. To her surprise, she didn't even feel overly concerned that she was wearing the bikini today. After all, she was in her own backyard. If this guy wanted to act so brazen, she was ready to stand her ground. Let him look!

She removed her hand from his and tipped her head slightly. "Do you always jump over neighbors' walls to make yourself known?" she calmly asked him.

He chuckled. "Not unless the neighbor is a hot babe like you."

Janelle groaned. "Now there's a great come-on line if I ever heard one."

Chelsea laughed. "Yes, Dayton. I think you need to work on that. Or maybe it's the delivery."

He looked slightly embarrassed. "So, uh, you're new in town?"

She nodded. "And you aren't?"

He looked like he didn't know what to say or what to do

with his hands, and since he had no pockets, he slipped them behind his back.

"Dayton is a senior," Janelle told Chelsea in a flat tone. "But I've known him since grade school. He used to be nicer."

"What year are you?" Dayton asked Chelsea.

"Junior." Chelsea smiled.

"That's cool." Dayton looked pleased, like he was relieved she was younger than him. "Very cool."

"Yeah, but don't get yourself all worked up, Hollywood, she's still out of your league," Janelle told him.

He threw his shoulders back. "Says who?"

Janelle laughed. "Anyone with a fully operative brain."

Dayton shook a finger at Janelle. "Wait a minute, Baby Face, how can she be out of my league if she's *your* friend?"

Janelle rolled her eyes, but she looked slightly uneasy.

He turned back to Chelsea. "Don't get pulled in by Baby Face. She might not have mentioned that she's just an academic geek."

Chelsea frowned at him. "So do you have something against intelligent girls?"

"Not if they come with a great package like you've got." He grinned.

"Thanks, but as I said . . ." Chelsea shifted to a cool tone. "It's a pleasure to meet you, Dayton. Now if you'll excuse us, Janelle and I were just going inside. We've had enough sun for a while."

"Hey, we were just getting acquainted," he said.

She gave him what she hoped looked like a bright but insincere smile. "Yes, we were. And it's been very nice, Dayton."

"I'd like to get to know you better, Chelsea," he said. "Maybe we could go and get—"

"Hopefully we will get to know each other better . . . some other time." She wiggled her fingers in a mini wave and stepped into the shade. "Really, you wouldn't want us to get sunstroke out here, would you?"

He gave a slightly goofy smile. "No, not at all. I gotta go anyway. I was on my way to football practice when I heard you girls talking and thought I'd sneak a peek." He stood straighter. "You probably don't know that I'm the starting quarterback this season."

Chelsea nodded like this was impressive. Really, it was. If the starting quarterback at her former school had even smiled at her, she would've been over the moon, but now . . . things were different. "Well, I wouldn't want to keep you from that, Dayton."

He grinned. "See you around then?"

"I hope so."

"Oh, brother," Janelle said after they were behind closed doors in the house. "What a jerk."

"Really?" Chelsea watched Dayton use a tree branch to hoist himself back to the top of the wall and over. "He was a little rude . . . but he seemed okay."

"Well, that just shows what you know. Or what you don't know. Trust me, Dayton Moore is a total jerk." She pointed to Chelsea and laughed. "But I don't know why I'm surprised."

Chelsea felt confused. "Why?"

"Because it's pretty obvious that you, Chelsea Martin, are a jerk magnet."

"A what?"

"A jerk magnet."

Chelsea frowned. She was trying hard not to feel offended, which wasn't easy. "What is that supposed to mean?"

Janelle was chortling even harder now. "I'm sorry, Chelsea." She let out a little snort of laughter. "I can't believe I actually said that. I mean, about being a jerk magnet—I suppose that sounds a little harsh."

"I guess."

"Although I do stand by what I said about Dayton. He is a first-class jerk, and I know lots of people who would agree with me on the subject."

"Fine!" Chelsea's voice grew sharp. "I wouldn't know about that since I barely met the guy. But why are you calling *me* a jerk magnet?" Suddenly she was rethinking her strategy to befriend this girl. Seriously, if this was how Janelle treated her friends, perhaps Chelsea needed to look elsewhere for connections.

"Really, I'm sorry, Chelsea." Janelle sputtered like she was attempting to control her laughter.

"Whatever." With narrowed eyes, Chelsea folded her arms across her front.

"I'm sorry," Janelle said again. "Please, forget I even said that. It was stupid, okay?"

"But I still want to know why you said it. I thought we were friends, and now you're treating me like—"

"Come here!" Janelle grabbed Chelsea by the arm and tugged her over to the mirror between the kitchen and dining area. "Look at yourself, Chelsea. Take a good long look."

Chelsea peered at her image. "What?"

"Just like Dayton said, you look like a hot babe, and to a jerk like him, a hot babe is like dangling raw meat in front of a hungry bear. Or in other words, a jerk magnet."

"Huh?" Chelsea wasn't sure if it was the mixed metaphors, too much time in the sun, or her own hurt feelings, but she was seriously baffled.

"And then you're wearing *that*." Janelle pointed at her chest.

Chelsea looked down at herself. "My bikini?"

"Talk about your first-rate jerk bait."

Chelsea slowly nodded. "Yeah, I sorta see what you mean. Maybe you're right." Still feeling defensive, not to mention hurt, she explained how Kate had given her the bikini as a going-away gift.

Janelle blinked. "I'll bet your dad loved that."

Chelsea chuckled. "Yeah . . . not so much." She confessed to Janelle about how she'd been wearing it when the college-aged guy had made a big pass at her in Albuquerque.

"See what I mean?" Janelle nodded triumphantly. "You are a jerk magnet."

"I'll admit this bikini isn't fit for public viewing. But to be fair, I was wearing it in the privacy—the so-called privacy—of my own backyard. First I get Chase gawking at me from your yard, and the next thing I know it's Dayton from the other side. Seriously, Janelle, what's a girl supposed to do?"

"I guess it's not really fair." Janelle grinned. "Unless you want to start wearing a burka."

"Yeah, right."

Janelle laughed. "Hey, I hear they have burka swimsuits that cover from head to toe."

"Sounds lovely."

They both started joking and laughing, and Chelsea told herself that Janelle hadn't meant to be mean when she'd called Chelsea a jerk magnet. Even so, it still stung a bit. In a way, it reminded her of how she'd felt blindsided by Virginia and her old friends. The way people could turn on you in an instant—it was scary.

After Janelle left, Chelsea took a good long look at herself in the full-length mirror with the bikini on. It did seem a bit indecent, especially considering that her own backyard wasn't as private as she'd imagined. She decided that from now on, she would forgo the bikini. That would make Dad happy too. Besides, it wasn't like the stringy pieces were particularly comfortable, even if the lack of tan lines was nice.

On Friday, Janelle and Chelsea went back-to-school shopping. The plan had been for Mrs. Parker to drive them, but at the last minute, Grayson stepped in and offered, explaining that he still needed to pick up a few things to take with him to college.

"He's just driving us because of you," Janelle whispered to Chelsea as they walked out to Janelle's mom's car. "He'll probably ask you to sit in front with him too." She made a disgusted face.

Chelsea shrugged. "So what do you want me to do about it?"

"We'll both just sit in back, okay?"

"Okay."

Janelle giggled. "We'll pretend Grayson's our chauffeur. That'll show him."

So when Grayson casually offered Chelsea the front seat, Janelle pulled her into the backseat. Calling her brother "James," Janelle commanded him like he was her personal servant, telling him what to do and how to get them to their destination. Grayson was actually a pretty good sport about it.

"Thank you, *James*," Janelle said as he pulled in front of the store. "But don't expect a bonus for today's driving performance."

"No problem," Grayson teased back. "I'll just drop you girls off here, and hopefully you can find another way to get home."

"You do that and I'll call Mom," Janelle threatened.

"Just kidding." Grayson held up his hands.

"We'll call you when we're ready to go," Janelle said as they got out.

"And just maybe I'll come and get you. That is, if I'm ready," he called through his open window.

"Thanks for the ride." Chelsea smiled at him. "For the record, I thought your driving skills were well above average."

He thanked her with a lopsided grin. "Maybe while I'm away at college, you can teach my sister some manners."

"I heard that, Grayson."

"Good." He nodded. "Take a hint."

Chelsea waved to him as she followed Janelle into the store. Last night Dad had informed her that a new shipment had come on Wednesday and that it had taken all of Thursday to get it put out. He'd also said that as long as she was discreet about it and handled the transaction herself, it would be okay for Janelle to get a few things on the employee discount.

They headed straight for the junior section, and remembering how Kate had perused the designer racks first, Chelsea made an attempt to imitate her. When she found something good, she'd take it over and hold it up in front of a full-length mirror. "This is the first step to shopping," she told Janelle. "You try to see if it even looks good on you. That way you don't waste time trying something on that's really not you."

"That makes sense." Janelle nodded. "See, you're better at this than you thought."

With that encouragement, Chelsea tried to remember more

of the shopping tips that Kate had taught her. The more she shared, the more her confidence grew. After they had both found a number of items and were in the dressing rooms trying things on, Chelsea heard a phone ringing in Janelle's changing room.

"Oh, Chase," Janelle said. "What's up?" She listened for a bit, then called over to Chelsea. "Chase wants to know if we're still on for the concert tomorrow night. Sounds like his dad got ahold of some free tickets."

Even though Chelsea was in her underwear, she popped out of her changing room and went into Janelle's. "Ask Chase if Nicholas is coming," she said in a whisper.

"Huh?"

"Ask about Nicholas, okay?"

Janelle shrugged. "Uh, Chase, is Nicholas coming?" She waited, then shrugged again.

"Tell him that I *want* Nicholas to come," Chelsea said. "Or else I'm not going." She lowered her voice. "That way Chase won't think that I'm on a date with him, okay?"

Janelle's eyes lit up, and she nodded eagerly. She relayed the message, and after a bit she hung up. "Chase said he'll get back to us on that." Janelle studied Chelsea. "Seriously, you think Nicholas will want to come too?"

Chelsea shrugged. "Why not?"

"I don't know." Janelle looked at Chelsea in her underwear. "You, uh, might want to go put something on."

They both giggled, and Chelsea hurried back to her changing room. She felt a little nervous about this plan. It was presumptuous of her to think that Nicholas would come just because she wanted him to. On the other hand, she seemed to have experienced some pretty impressive success at turning guys' heads lately. Why shouldn't she turn Nicholas's?

Shortly after the girls had finalized their selections, made their purchases, and were waiting for Grayson to pick them up, Chase called again. To Chelsea's surprise, Janelle handed the phone to her. "Fine. Here she is," she said in a flat tone.

"I just wanted to tell you that Nicholas has agreed to come, Chelsea. So I wanted to be sure this wasn't some kind of trick on Janelle's part. Are you really coming now?"

"Sure, I'm coming." She tossed Janelle a look.

"Oh, well, cool."

"See ya then." Chelsea handed the phone back to Janelle.

"Are you happy now?" Janelle asked him. A few more words were exchanged, then Janelle hung up, rolling her eyes. "Chase can be so obnoxious." She shook her head as she dropped her phone in her purse. "I honestly don't know what I even see in him."

"Maybe you're a jerk magnet too," Chelsea teased.

"Huh?" Janelle frowned.

"You're the magnet that's attracted to the jerk. Not the other way around."

"Very funny." Janelle scowled then laughed. "But I suppose you could be right. Maybe it is a two-way street."

Chelsea nodded. She felt slightly vindicated now. It had been bugging her that Janelle had called her a jerk magnet yesterday. But if they were both jerk magnets—perhaps one was a north pole and the other a south pole—maybe it wasn't so insulting after all.

twelve

Chelsea was well aware that she spent more time getting ready for things than she'd ever spent before. Part of her felt a little silly about this new self-absorption and the primping and preening that came with it. But another part of her didn't care. After all, how many years had she put zero effort into her appearance? Back then, instead of focusing on how great she could look, Chelsea had been preoccupied with making herself as invisible as possible. It was funny how obsessions could change.

She finally decided on an outfit she'd tried on before the pile of clothes on her bed had become a small mountain. She knew wearing white jeans was risky—one spill and she could be a mess—but she also knew she looked hot in these jeans. And with the watermelon-red top, which showed off her curves, and a woven Prada belt that she'd gotten for next to nothing, she was smoking. She was tempted to take a phone photo and send it to Kate just to impress her, but it was almost time to go, and she still wanted to touch up her makeup. Over the top? Maybe so. But more than anything, she wanted to catch Nicholas Prague's eye tonight.

She knew this wasn't a date per se, but in her mind, she imagined it was. Because Chase had promised to get Nicholas to come, she felt reasonably sure that he'd be with them tonight. All day long she'd been practicing conversations she might have with him. She had questions all ready to ask him. And she planned to do whatever was necessary, within reason, to turn that boy's head. She wasn't sure if what she was experiencing was truly a crush or not, but she knew she was pretty much obsessed with Nicholas Prague. The question was, could she get him to return the obsession?

Dad let out a whistle as Chelsea walked through the great room. "Wowzers, Chels, you look—well, uh—" he stammered.

She stared back at him. "Is something wrong?"

"No." He shook his head. "You look very pretty. You say this is a Christian concert you're going to?"

She nodded as she slipped her purse over her shoulder. "Like I said, there are a bunch of kids from Janelle's church all going together."

Dad was turned away from her, looking out the front window. "So this isn't a date or anything like that?"

"No," she assured him. "It's not a date. Just kids doing something together." She went over to stand by him. "But what if it was a date?"

He turned and looked at her with one brow arched slightly. "Then I'd say it's time for us to have a father-daughter talk, young lady."

She laughed. "What would you tell me?"

"Oh, the regular stuff. I'd warn you that all teenage boys have one thing and one thing only on their minds."

"Oh, Dad!" She shook her head. "Do you really believe that?"

"You bet I do."

"What about nice churchgoing boys?"

He frowned. "They're probably the worst of the bunch."

"The worst?" She acted shocked. However, she remembered the way Chase had come on to her, how he'd looked at her . . . and she wasn't so sure that Dad wasn't right.

"You've turned into a very, very pretty girl," Dad said. "I just hope that you're well aware—" He stopped and pointed to a white van in front of the house with the church's name on the side of it. "Is that what you're going in?"

She chuckled. "I guess so. One guy's dad is the pastor."

Dad looked relieved. "It looks like there are a bunch of kids already in there." He turned and smiled at her. "Well, you have fun now."

"Thanks." Chelsea was already going out the door.

"And you've got your phone if you need anything."

"Yes, Dad." She waved and closed the door. As she walked toward the van, she pasted a smile on her face, trying to hide her disappointment. She'd hoped that it would only be Chase and Janelle and Nicholas and her, but her dad was right. The van was already nearly filled with kids.

"Hey," Janelle called as she jogged across her yard toward them.

"I didn't know that Chase was bringing half the youth group with him," Chelsea said.

Janelle laughed. "The more the merrier, I guess."

Chase jumped out of the van, holding the side door open

for them. "Welcome, ladies." He gave Chelsea a big smile. "Welcome, welcome!"

Raymond was in the driver's seat, with Nicholas sitting next to him. Both called out greetings as she and Janelle slid into the middle seat. Chelsea recognized some of the other faces but couldn't quite get the names.

"Let's rock 'n' roll," Chase called as he closed the door and popped into the seat next to Janelle. At least that was a relief. Yet Chelsea couldn't help but feel a sense of letdown as the van full of youth group kids drove through town. People were laughing and joking and singing, but feeling out of place and a bit silly for her high expectations, she kept her gaze fixed out the window. Except for every once in a while when she let herself glance at Nicholas. He looked even more hand-some tonight than he had at the barbecue. From this angle, with those cheekbones and straight nose, he reminded her of Orlando Bloom.

With the noise in the van, she couldn't make out what Nicholas and Raymond were saying, but they seemed to be in the midst of an intense conversation about something. She was trying to listen, but then Nicholas looked back at her and she felt rather intrusive. For a moment their eyes locked and she felt a rush of pleasure. But then his brow creased in a way that suggested he was displeased about something—most likely that she was eavesdropping. Suddenly feeling insecure, she quickly looked away out of habit.

As the van continued its drive, she kept her eyes and ears tuned in to everything going on outside. She felt as much like a misfit as she'd ever felt, and she wondered if she'd ever fit in . . . anywhere. Maybe it was her destiny to be an outsider. Maybe she should simply expect it.

Finally they were at the megachurch where the concert was being held. Happy to escape the slightly claustrophobic van, Chelsea stood by herself, waiting for the kids to reassemble and head into the concert. She was slightly surprised to see that Nicholas seemed to be pairing up with a girl named Olivia Hutchison. Olivia seemed like a nice girl, although she was pretty loud, but she was also quite chubby and, in Chelsea's opinion, not very pretty or fashionable. Naturally, Chelsea felt curious as to how this frumpy-dumpy girl had attracted someone as hot as Nicholas.

"Hey, good lookin'." Chase came over and linked arms with Chelsea, loudly singing the old ditty. "Whatcha got cookin'? How's about cookin'—"

"Good grief, Chase." Janelle frowned at him as she linked his other arm with hers. "Could you be any more obnoxious?"

"Obnoxious?" He gave her an innocent look. "Hey, I'm just being friendly."

Chelsea actually appreciated this token of attention. Feeling more and more like the outsider, she was happy to feel included by someone, even if it was only Chase. She just hoped that it wouldn't make Janelle jealous.

After they got inside the church's foyer, Janelle tugged Chelsea toward the women's restroom. "Why aren't you being more friendly to Nicholas?" she whispered as she paused by the drinking fountain.

"What do you mean?"

Janelle gave her a "duh" look. "I know you like him."

"So?" Chelsea shrugged.

"So, go after him."

"How am I supposed to do that?" Chelsea asked.

"Just go up and talk to him," Janelle suggested.

"Just like that?"

Janelle shrugged. "Why not? You look great—as usual. Chase can't keep his eyes off you. Why not use what you've got to get Nicholas to pay attention too?"

Chelsea twisted her mouth to one side. That had originally been her plan, but now she wasn't so sure.

"Come on," Janelle urged, "give it your best shot. I'm sure Nicholas has no idea that you like him. Take the initiative." Chase was waving at them like it was time to find their seats. Janelle hurried to join him, and Chelsea glanced around to see that Nicholas was still with Olivia. Bolstering her spirits, she decided to take Janelle's advice and just go for it. Really, what did she have to lose? Well, besides her pride.

"Hey there, Olivia," Chelsea said as she joined the two of them. "I think I met you at the barbecue, but we didn't really get a chance to talk. I'm new in town and trying to get to know some people." Chelsea carefully avoided Nicholas's eyes.

Olivia smiled. "Yeah, I remember you." She gave what seemed an approving nod. "You look really pretty tonight."

Chelsea kind of shrugged. "Thanks. So do you."

Olivia's smile faded a bit. "Thanks." She glanced at Nicholas. "You probably already know Chelsea, right?"

"We met before," he said in a slightly chilly tone.

"That's right." Chelsea nodded. "You spoke at the barbecue. I really liked what you said."

He brightened some. "Thanks. That's nice to hear."

"I wanted to tell you that night," she continued. "But you were already surrounded by your adoring fans."

Now his smile looked a little stiff.

"Yes, Nicholas does attract some followers." Olivia's tone was edged with sarcasm. "Especially of the female variety."

She chuckled but looked directly at Chelsea. "You should've seen this guy at camp. All the girls there fell madly in love with him. Didn't they, Nick?"

He shrugged and glanced away. "Not so I noticed."

"Poor Nick." Olivia put her arm around his shoulders in a sideways hug. "He tries to be nice to everyone. But the girls just seem to take him the wrong way. Well, most of the girls anyway."

"That must be a challenge." Chelsea pressed her lips together, trying to think of a graceful way to get out of this. Olivia obviously thought Chelsea was no different than those other girls. Even though it was true, Chelsea had no desire to stand here feeling foolish.

"You have to give Nick credit," Olivia continued. "He tries to keep a low profile, but the girls are like flies to honey whenever he's around."

"Like flies to honey?" He laughed. "Give me a break, Olivia."

"It's true and you know it."

"Well . . . I, uh, I just wanted to say hi." Chelsea stepped away. "I think I'll go find a seat." Before Olivia could make another insinuation, Chelsea hurried down the aisle and as far away from them as she could get. As a result, she wound up sitting near the front with people she'd never met. She could feel the heat of embarrassment on her face, but she simply leaned over, put her head in her hands, and tried to gather her thoughts, hoping that others would assume she was praying.

She felt perfectly ridiculous. She couldn't believe how much effort and energy she'd put into this evening. How she'd thought it might be almost like a date and that she'd somehow manage to get Nicholas's attention. Well, she'd gotten it all right. Now she was so embarrassed she didn't care if she ever crossed paths with him again. And that Olivia—well, she was a real piece of work. *Like flies to honey?* Who says that? But what really got Chelsea was how Olivia seemed perfectly confident and self-assured in her own skin. How had that happened? Chelsea simply did not get it.

The music was already playing, and Chelsea had to admit that the band seemed pretty good. Of course, she felt out of sync with everyone else smiling and singing, clapping and swaying to the beat. But she reminded herself that she was working on her acting skills. Why not put them to use here? So she began to act as if she were having as good a time as anyone. Ironically, the more she pretended, the less she needed to. She actually was enjoying herself.

But it was more than that. Chelsea felt as if the words to the songs and the messages being shared by the musicians were going straight to her heart. The more she heard about how these people were experiencing real relationships with a living God and how Jesus wanted to be their friend—their very best friend—the more she wanted this exact same thing in her own life. Chelsea knew she'd been lonely for a long time—probably since the death of her mother—and she wanted a friend who would stick by her no matter what.

When it came time to accept the challenge to step out of her comfort zone and go forward to stand up near the band, Chelsea went. With trembling knees and tears streaking down her cheeks, she prayed the prayer with the others who were standing up front.

"Dear Jesus," she echoed the girl who was leading them, "thank you for forgiving me . . . I ask you to come into my heart . . . I invite you into my life . . . Thank you for wanting to be my best friend." Finally she said, "Amen."

The music started again, and people slowly filed back

to their seats. As Chelsea made her way back, she glanced around to see if any others from the youth group had come up here, but she didn't recognize any faces. Probably those kids had long since made this kind of commitment. That was fine because Chelsea knew that what she'd done was between her and God.

For the next few songs, the lyrics were posted on a huge screen behind the podium, which made it easy for Chelsea to sing along. As she sang these worshipful songs, she realized that she honestly meant the words. This was no act. She didn't fully understand what she'd signed up for, but she knew the commitment she'd just made was genuine. And although she had no idea where all this would take her, she didn't feel worried. Mostly she was just happy. Not a delirious, over-the-top sort of happy—it was more of a quiet and expectant kind of happy. Peaceful.

She sat in the same seat in the van as they drove home. This time everyone in the van was louder and more boister-ous than earlier. Chelsea felt a bit like the old Chelsea . . . the invisible wallflower. But oddly enough, this time she didn't really mind. She just wanted to be quiet and to soak all this in. She wanted to think about everything, to absorb what had happened tonight, to hide it deep inside of her—almost as if it were a rare jewel, something precious that she needed to protect and hold on to.

thirteen

Just when Chelsea felt like she'd gained a somewhat secure position in Janelle's life, almost best friend status, Lishia Vance returned from her summer vacation. Lishia, it seemed, was Janelle's real best friend. This was only alluded to when Janelle suddenly became unavailable because she was with Lishia, then soundly driven home when Janelle brought Lishia over to meet Chelsea.

With just days before school was scheduled to begin, the three girls were hanging by the pool, like Chelsea assumed friends might do, but Lishia seemed determined to turn their conversation into some sort of competition between her and Chelsea. Every time Chelsea said anything, no matter how trivial, it felt like Lishia had to say something better to top her. Like Lishia thought someone was keeping score. Even when Chelsea casually mentioned to Janelle that a new shipment of designer jeans had just arrived at Best 4 Less, she was cut off mid-sentence.

"Oh, Chelsea," Lishia gushed, "you should see the clothes my grandmother got me when we were in New York City." Off she went describing each individual item of clothing in painstaking detail. Chelsea didn't even think the clothes sounded that great, not to her anyway. But the most aggravating part was that when Lishia talked, which was often, it felt like Chelsea wasn't even there . . . or was invisible. Even when she stood and picked up their empty drink glasses and went into the house, no one seemed to notice.

Chelsea puttered around in the house for a bit. She didn't want to seem like a rude hostess, but how much was she expected to take from Lishia? Finally Janelle and Lishia came inside.

"Thanks for letting us come over," Janelle told her.

Chelsea forced a smile. "Sure . . . anytime."

"Yeah, thanks," Lishia said halfheartedly.

"Lishia's mom's picking her up in a few minutes," Janelle said.

"She promised to take us to the mall." Lishia tugged on Janelle's arm. "Come on, we better hurry if we want to get changed."

Janelle gave Chelsea an apologetic glance. Chelsea just smiled like it was no problem. "Have fun," she called out as they left. But after they were gone, she felt like crying. A hard lump grew in her throat, and she remembered what Virginia had done to her. Even though it was so long ago, it felt familiar and close now. As she wiped down the kitchen countertops, that old loneliness settled on her like a damp, gray cloud.

She poured soap into the dishwasher and reminded herself

that she had God in her life now. He was her new best friend. She'd been praying to him too. God would get her through this. But as she turned the dishwasher on, she wondered—if Janelle and Lishia were Christians (since they were part of the youth group), didn't that mean they should act differently? Or was Chelsea just assuming things? She felt confused as she picked up some newspapers and tidied up the great room. How were Christians supposed to act? How was she supposed to act? Was there someone to ask or some kind of guidebook somewhere?

She went back outside to check on the pool chemicals and do some vacuuming. Dad had made it clear from the get-go that keeping the pool clean was her job, and she took it seriously. She didn't mind the work, especially now when she needed something to distract her from feeling left out. She was trying to untwist the pool's vacuum hose when she noticed Dayton waving to her from the top of the wall between their properties.

"Need any help over there?" he called.

She shrugged. "I'm okay."

He hopped down onto her side. "You're more than okay," he said, coming over. Leaning over the surface of the pool, he reached out to grab and untangle the hose, and without even asking, he started to help her. He chatted congenially as he assisted her in cleaning the pool and moving things around as they scrubbed the surrounding deck. To her surprise, she enjoyed his company. It seemed some of his previous cockiness had disappeared. In fact, he was almost polite.

"You seem different today," she told him as they were stowing tools back in the pool shed. "Nicer."

He chuckled. "Probably because Janelle's not here."

"You really don't like her?" Chelsea studied his expression.

He shrugged. "She's probably okay, but she and some of the other academics can be, you know, a little obnoxious."

"I suppose you and your friends are never obnoxious."

He grinned. "I guess some might think we are."

"Well, at least you're honest." She closed the door to the shed. "Thanks for your help."

"No problem." He cocked his head to one side. "So what do you think? Would you be interested in doing something with me?"

"Like what?"

"I don't know . . . like go grab a burger or something?"

She considered this. She actually was hungry. "You mean right now?"

His eyes lit up. "Sure. I haven't even had lunch yet. How about heading to Bergdorf Burgers?"

"Bergdorf Burgers?"

"Yeah."

"Do they make designer burgers?"

He shrugged. "I don't know. Bernie Bergdorf opened it a couple years ago. And it's pretty good. You in?"

"Okay, but how do we get there?"

"I'll drive us."

She remembered what Dad had told her about California's driving law. "But I thought teens weren't allowed to drive other teens unless—"

He grinned. "I just turned eighteen."

"So you're legal?"

He nodded. "Totally legal."

She realized she was still in her swimsuit. Fortunately, it wasn't the bikini this time. "Let me run and change."

He looked slightly disappointed. "Not on my account."

She rolled her eyes. "On my account."

"Okay. I'll get my car and come around to pick you up. Like ten minutes?"

"Perfect."

He looked surprised. "Really?"

"Sure, why not?"

"I, uh, I just never knew a girl who could get ready in ten minutes."

She stuck out her hand. "Well, you met one now."

"Cool!"

She hurried inside, wondering if she really could get ready in ten minutes. In the old days, no problem . . . but now? Still, it was a fun test, and it eliminated the chance to be too choosy, which in some ways felt good. She pulled on some khaki shorts and a white T-shirt, ran a brush through her hair, and put on a little lip gloss and mascara. As she shoved her feet into her sandals, she thought that Dayton could take her or leave her—really, it made no difference since she wasn't that into him. Oh, there was no denying that his attention was flattering, but she had no interest in getting involved with a sports jock.

When she went outside to where Dayton was standing next to a shiny blue late-model Mustang, she thought he looked like a cliché. But when he grinned at her like he thought she looked like a million bucks, she had to wonder—maybe Dayton had more going on than she realized. Anyway, what was the harm in finding out?

"I never saw a chick eat like you do," he told her as she polished off her burger.

She wasn't sure if she should be offended or not.

"No offense." He held up his hands. "I mean, I like it."

"Oh." She nodded and reached for a fry. "Well, I was hungry. I kind of skimped on breakfast, then I swam laps this morning and—"

"You swam laps?" He looked surprised.

"Sure. I do most mornings. It's good exercise."

"Yeah, I know." He looked at her like he was trying to figure her out. "I just never knew a girl like that."

She laughed. "You mean one who's not afraid to eat good food or swim laps?"

He was still studying her. "Uh-huh."

She considered confessing all to him, then stopped herself. Really, what difference did it make? Especially when it seemed that he liked her as she was.

As they continued to talk, it seemed that he had dropped his previous facade and even admitted that he was worried about getting into a good college next year. "My mom is all sure that I can get an athletic scholarship, but I know that's probably not going to happen—not at a big school anyway. I might act like I'm all that, but I'm aware that guys like me are easy to come by."

"You never know."

He shrugged. "I've got a feeling. Plus I know my grades aren't real impressive. Probably because I've been more focused on sports than books."

"It's weird, isn't it?"

"What?" He looked curious.

"How high school doesn't really get us ready for what's out there. And then we turn eighteen and we're supposed to figure it out for ourselves."

He nodded. "Yeah, and I'm already eighteen. Who knows

where I'll be a year from now." He nodded toward the kitchen. "I could be in there flipping burgers. I'd probably have to work full time just to pay for my car."

"You bought the car yourself?" For some reason, she'd assumed it was a gift.

"My dad got it for me when I turned sixteen. I know it's because my parents divorced when I was a kid and my dad's trying to make up for some stuff. But he made it clear to me that unless I take over all the payments and insurance and everything after I graduate, I'll have to say adios to the Mustang." He sighed. "It's a sweet little ride."

"Too bad."

He shook his head like he was trying to wake up. "Sorry! I don't know why I'm going on about all that depressing biz. Man, you probably won't ever want to go out with me again."

She felt guilty now, thinking how she hadn't wanted to go out with him in the first place. "I've enjoyed this," she told him. "I like it when people aren't afraid to just be themselves." Of course, she felt somewhat hypocritical since she was getting so used to keeping her own guard up. But that was different.

"That's cool." He nodded. "Maybe that's why I like you."

"Thanks."

"Well, that and because you're easy on the eyes." He grinned.

"This has been fun." She set her wadded-up napkin in the burger basket and smiled.

"Fun enough that you'd do it again?"

She pressed her lips together. "Maybe so."

As they rode home, Dayton asked if Janelle had told her about Riley yet.

"Who?"

"Riley Atkins. She used to be my girlfriend. I figured Janelle might've blabbed to you about her."

"No, she didn't mention it."

"Well, Riley and I went out for most of last year. She broke up with me right after prom. Some of my buddies said she only stayed with me to go to the stupid dance." He shrugged. "Maybe they're right."

"Oh."

"Riley is full of herself, like the world revolves around her—or like it should. I mean, just because a girl is pretty and popular doesn't mean she should treat everyone else like—" His speech degenerated into some pretty coarse language. After a bit he seemed to notice that Chelsea wasn't responding, and he looked slightly embarrassed. "Sorry, I didn't mean to go on like that. But if I get to thinking or talking about that girl . . . well, I just can't help myself."

"It's hard when people hurt you."

"I guess. And I know Riley's not worth feeling bad over. But with school starting . . . well, I'm not looking forward to seeing her."

Chelsea could relate to this. She knew it was totally different, but she vividly remembered how she felt whenever September rolled around, how much she hated returning to school. She'd even begged to be homeschooled a couple of times. "Well, fortunately for you, I'm sure you have lots of other friends."

He nodded, then turned to look at her. "But you're new at school. Do you know anyone besides Janelle?"

"Her friend Lishia."

Dayton made a sour face.

Chelsea chuckled. "And Lishia doesn't seem to like me much."

"I'm not surprised."

"Why?" She felt defensive. "I was perfectly nice to her."

"That's not it. You know how girls can be."

Okay, now he had her. She wasn't sure she did know. Oh, she'd known at one point, sort of . . . but that was a long time ago.

"Girls can be so petty and jealous. Riley and her friends were always competing—over everything. I swear they're worse than guys sometimes. Except they're all quiet about it. They sugarcoat it or else they talk behind each other's backs. It's seriously twisted."

Chelsea laughed. "Yes, I do know what you mean."

"But you don't seem like that."

"Thanks. That's how I hope to keep it."

He pulled up to her house. "If you need a ride to school or anything—I mean, I have practice afterwards, so I couldn't bring you home. But if you needed a ride, like even on the first day, I'd be more than willing to pick you up."

"Thanks. I might take you up on that offer."

"Do you think you'd be interested in doing anything this weekend?" He looked hopeful.

"Maybe so. Although I'm not sure what my dad's plans are . . . or if he has any." Despite her initial resolve, she gave Dayton her phone number. It wasn't that she was crushing on him or anything like that, but he seemed like a pretty nice guy—underneath his star quarterback veneer. As she got out of the car and waved at him, she realized she no longer cared what Janelle thought of him. After all, Janelle had Lishia.

fourteen

The first week of school was nothing like Chelsea had expected. For starters, everyone seemed to assume that she was Dayton Moore's new girlfriend. Now, while Chelsea hadn't done anything to squelch this rumor, she wasn't exactly comfortable with it either. But hanging with Dayton seemed preferable to being friendless and alone. Thanks to Lishia, Janelle seemed to be keeping Chelsea at arm's length.

Even though Chelsea had followed Janelle's suggestion from a couple weeks ago to sign up for drama, and even though she had that class with Janelle, it seemed that Janelle was determined to treat Chelsea like she was contagious.

"Excuse me," Chelsea finally said to Janelle on Friday afternoon. They were going into the auditorium at the same time, the location of their drama class. "I think maybe we've met before."

Janelle's brows arched. "You're talking to *me*?"

Chelsea continued her little charade. "Yes, you seem rather familiar. Do you perhaps live in the same neighborhood?"

Janelle seemed honestly surprised. "Huh?"

"Why have you been acting like this?" Chelsea quietly asked her.

"Me?" Janelle gave her an innocent look.

Chelsea shrugged. "Oh, I suppose it was me snubbing you. Right?"

Janelle nodded like she honestly believed this nonsense.

"Are you serious?"

"Let's take the seats back there." Janelle pointed to the seats in the rear of the auditorium where the class met.

Once they were seated, Chelsea continued trying to get to the bottom of Janelle's snooty behavior, but the more they talked, the more it seemed obvious that Janelle had been thinking the exact same things about Chelsea.

"But what have I done?" Chelsea demanded. "I smile and say hi to you, and you act like you're blind and deaf or you—"

"Because I know you're just *pretending* to be nice."

"*Pretending?*" Chelsea stared at her. "What are you—"

"Now that you've got your new hoity-toity set of friends, you're too high and mighty for me and my friends and—"

"That is so not true!"

"Lishia told me how you snubbed her in English—"

"I have *never* snubbed her!" Chelsea seethed. "But she's snubbed me ever since I first met her. Even that day at my house when she—"

"Excuse me up there in the back row." Mr. Valotti waved from the stage. "Why don't you two girls bring your discussion down here to the stage for everyone to hear?"

"Sorry," Janelle called back.

Chelsea just nodded.

"No, I mean it," he insisted, "you two girls come down here, please."

Chelsea and Janelle exchanged glances, then got up. Amid comments and teasing from the rest of the class, they made their way down the stairs and onto the stage.

"Sorry about that," Chelsea mumbled to the teacher.

He smiled at her. "Remind me of your name."

"Chelsea Martin."

"You're a new student, right?"

She just nodded.

"Have you been in any productions before?"

"Just behind the scenes." She briefly explained her minor responsibilities at her previous drama classes.

"That's great to hear," he said, "because I usually expect new students to learn the ropes, so to speak, by working on lights, makeup, and costumes. But since you've already been there and done that, I'm sure you'll have no problems with auditioning."

"Auditioning?"

"For a role in our fall production."

"Oh." She glanced nervously at Janelle.

"As you all know," he said loudly to everyone, "we're doing *The Man Who Came to Dinner* for our fall play. As usual, it's not a musical. We'll wait until spring for that." He nodded to the stacks of scripts piled on the edge of the stage. "For those of you who plan to audition, come on up here and get a script." He looked back at Chelsea. "You get one too. I want you to audition for the role of Maggie."

"Maggie?"

"Are you familiar with this play?"

"No, I don't think so."

"That's fine. You will be." He turned to Janelle. "I'm not sure which role you'll want to audition for, but I'm sure you'll figure something out. Now if everyone will begin finding their seats, I will tell you a bit about this charming old play, which is fun for Christmas. For anyone who's unfamiliar with the story, you're invited to join me to watch the 1942 film version after school today at 3:30."

Chelsea and Janelle found new seats, not in the back this time, and listened as Mr. Valotti discoursed on the play and how it was produced first on the stage, later by Hollywood, and finally on television.

"Are you going to watch the video today?" Janelle asked Chelsea as class ended.

"I think so."

"Me too."

"Do you want to finish our conversation?" Chelsea asked a bit tentatively.

Janelle nodded, and they agreed to meet after school and go to the movie together.

They were just turning toward the math department when Dayton stopped Chelsea. "Hey, you never told me if you're coming to the game tonight or not." He smiled hopefully. "You will come, won't you?"

She explained about the movie after school.

"When will it get done?"

"I assume it's a couple hours. Like 5:30 maybe?"

"Want me to pick you up then?"

"Sure, that'd be great."

"The varsity game doesn't start until eight. But if you want to ride with me, we'll have to go early. You'll have to watch part of the JV game."

She wanted to point out that she hadn't committed to going to the game yet. "I need to get to class," she said as the warning bell rang.

"See you around 5:30 then, in front of the school."

Janelle gave Chelsea a doubtful look, as if she questioned her judgment. Chelsea simply smiled and said she'd see her later. As she headed for class, she caught Dayton's ex-girlfriend, Riley Atkins, dressed in her blue and red cheerleader's uniform and scowling at her. It wasn't the first time this had happened either. For whatever reason, it seemed that she now resented Chelsea, which was hard to imagine since Riley had been the one to break up with Dayton. Plus she didn't even know Chelsea.

As Chelsea slipped into a desk, she realized that all she wanted was a friend. Just one loyal and good and dependable friend. She knew that God was her friend, and that was great, but someone wearing skin would be nice too. Ironically, it seemed the only available and willing candidate was Dayton. Every time she turned around, he was there. Ready with a friendly smile, encouraging word, or a needed ride, Dayton came through. Even if his motives were selfish—and she had no doubt that sometimes they were—it was still a comfort to know he was there for her.

After school, she and Janelle got sodas and slowly walked over to where Mr. Valotti planned to show the movie. As they walked, they talked, and the more Janelle talked, the more Chelsea began to suspect that Lishia had been very manipulative.

"I kind of thought you might be using me this summer," Janelle finally said, "but when school started, it seemed pretty obvious."

"What seems obvious is that Lishia wants to make sure I don't come between you and her." Chelsea sighed. "I can't really blame her. Good friends are hard to come by. But even if you don't have room for another friend in your life, and even if Lishia can't stand me, which I suspect is the case, it would still be nice not to feel like I'm your enemy." Chelsea felt a lump in her throat.

"Is that how you feel?"

Chelsea shrugged. "Kind of. I mean, you've pretty much been ignoring me."

"I just thought you were so busy with Dayton." Janelle shook her head. "And to be honest, I can't figure that out. Dayton is such a—"

"Dayton has been a friend to me. Just about the only one I have."

"But you know what he's after, don't you?"

"Of course. I know he wants this relationship to turn into something more than what I want."

Janelle looked confused. "Meaning you don't consider yourself his girlfriend?"

Chelsea laughed. "No. And Dayton knows that."

Janelle's expression was skeptical.

Chelsea decided to tell Janelle about the commitment she'd made to God at the concert. "I don't know exactly what that means, but I'd like to get more involved in a youth group. I'd hoped maybe yours, but now I'm thinking I might not be welcome there. I asked Dayton if he ever went to church, and he just laughed. But he said he might go to church if I took him. That's pretty funny considering I don't even have a church to go to. Talk about the blind leading the blind."

Janelle looked truly stunned. To Chelsea's surprise, she hugged her. "I'm so sorry, Chelsea. I've been a totally rotten friend to you. Please forgive me!"

Chelsea hugged her back. "I just think you got influenced by someone who doesn't really know me." They stepped back and looked at each other. "I'm not saying that Lishia purposely maligned me . . ." Of course, she wasn't going to say that Lishia hadn't either.

"Lishia has always been kind of jealous."

"I meant what I said before," Chelsea reminded her. "I don't want to replace Lishia. I respect that you two are best friends. I'd just like to be your friend too."

"You are my friend, Chelsea."

"Hey, friends," Mr. Valotti said cheerfully, "how about coming in for the film?"

Chelsea smiled at him. "That's why we're here."

"I'll be curious to see what you think of Maggie. She's played by Bette Davis."

"Bette Davis?" Chelsea said, feeling more interested now. "You know who that is?"

"Of course." Chelsea nodded. "I *love* Bette Davis."

"You do?" He looked dubious.

"*All About Eve* is one of my favorite old movies."

"Really?" he said. "That's a great classic."

Suddenly they were talking about Bette Davis and old movies, and Janelle was looking at Chelsea with a mixed expression of curiosity and concern. When Mr. Valotti invited Chelsea to sit next to him, she urged Janelle to sit on the other side. As the movie played, he quietly pointed several things out to them.

"See that fire in her eye," he whispered to Chelsea. "That's what you'll need to capture to carry out that role. She's a spicy one."

Janelle gently elbowed Chelsea, but when Chelsea turned

to look at her, Janelle's eyes were fixed on the screen and her arms were folded across her front as if she were irked about something.

To Chelsea's surprise, Mr. Valotti asked her to remain and discuss the part of Maggie after the movie ended. "I'm sorry," she told him. "My ride is probably waiting for me." She smiled. "Another time, okay?"

"Okay." He nodded and smiled.

Chelsea hurried to catch up with Janelle. "What's the hurry?"

"Too hot and heavy in there." Janelle shook her head.

"Huh?"

"I can't believe Mr. Valotti was flirting with you."

"What?" Chelsea grabbed Janelle by the forearm, stopping her in her tracks.

Janelle looked directly into her eyes. "You seriously didn't get that?"

"No." Chelsea shook her head. "I think you're imagining things."

"Oh, Chelsea, you are *so* oblivious."

"I thought we were going to be friends." Chelsea felt blindsided again. "Why are you saying things like that? Don't you know it hurts?"

"I said that because I think it's the truth. And friends tell each other the truth, right?" They began walking again.

"Well, here's my truth, Janelle. What you just said is insulting to me. It's like you think I'm a slut or—"

"No, no, you don't get it. It's not you, Chelsea. Not exactly anyway. It's the guys who are being jerks. But it's like you send out some signal . . . like what I said before. You're a jerk magnet."

Chelsea looked over her shoulder, then spoke quietly. "So are you saying Mr. Valotti is a jerk?"

Janelle pressed her lips together and slowly shook her head. "You know, I'd heard rumors, but until today I'd never actually seen anything. Now I'm starting to wonder."

"Oh, Janelle." Chelsea felt disappointed. "I can't believe you'd say that."

"I'm serious."

They were at the front door, and Dayton's car was already waiting. "Do you need a ride?" Chelsea asked.

"With Dayton?" Janelle laughed loudly. "No way. My mom's picking me up. But we can give you a ride."

Chelsea waved at Dayton. "Thanks, but since Dayton made the effort to come get me, the least I can do is ride with him. Another time, okay?"

"What does your dad think of Dayton?"

Chelsea shrugged. "He's fine with him. I mean, they barely met the other day. Why?"

"Just curious."

Chelsea paused with one hand on the door. "So . . . we're still friends then?"

"Absolutely." Janelle nodded. "But as your friend, I will tell you the truth. Okay?"

"Okay."

"I'll try to do it more gently though."

"I'd appreciate that." Chelsea told her goodbye, then jogged out to get in the car.

"How was the flick?" Dayton asked as she buckled her seat belt.

"Pretty cute." She told him about how she wanted to try out for a part. "Mr. Valotti thinks I can do it."

Dayton tossed a sideways glance at her. "Is Mr. Valotti coming on to you?"

She laughed nervously. "Of course not. Why would you say that?"

"Because that man has a reputation."

She brushed this off, but she was starting to wonder.

fifteen

The second week of school showed some signs of improvement for Chelsea. Although she was trying to keep things cool and calm between her and Dayton, she could tell that he was getting impatient. She could also tell that he wanted everyone to think they were a couple. In a way, that was sweet. In another way, it was disturbing.

However, it was not as disturbing as the way Nicholas Prague was treating her. After attending youth group on Saturday night with Janelle and a slightly irritable Lishia, Chelsea had hoped that other members of the church group would become more accepting of her. Of course, Chase was always glad to see her. Not that it helped her friendship with Janelle much, since she still seemed to be pining for him.

Perhaps Chelsea's biggest social success had been initiating a somewhat shaky friendship with Olivia Hutchison. Although they had economics together, Olivia had been a bit chilly at first, but Chelsea remained persistent and eventually Olivia warmed up.

"You're a lot nicer than I thought you were," Olivia finally told her on Friday.

"And you're even funnier than I thought you were," Chelsea said. "I seriously think you could do stand-up and get rich."

"Thanks!" Olivia beamed, but then her smile faded. "The truth is I'd trade my humor for your looks."

Chelsea shook her head as they left the classroom. "Looks are highly overrated. And someday, when we have time, I can tell you why."

"Really?" Olivia looked hopeful.

As predicted, Chelsea had gotten the role of Maggie in the play. But now she was concerned that Janelle, and Dayton as well, might've been right about Mr. Valotti. Oh, he hadn't actually done anything morally questionable. But he was definitely a touchy-feely sort of guy, and sometimes the implications seemed clear, even to someone as oblivious as her. As a result, she felt like she needed to keep a safe distance and watch her step, but being on her guard like that felt restrictive. And then she'd second-guess herself, wondering if her suspicions had more to do with what she'd heard than what she'd actually experienced firsthand. Sometimes being attractive felt like a tricky tightrope dance. She wondered if she'd ever figure out how to act like a normal person.

However, the most frustrating part of her fledgling social life was Nicholas Prague. It wasn't that she'd expected him to fall madly in love with her. Not after the night of the concert anyway. But he'd been so cold to her the first week of school that she wondered if there was some reason he detested her. Had she done something offensive? She was working hard to eliminate her crush on him, but she was learning the hard way that the heat of a crush is a hard thing to extinguish.

She wished she'd never allowed herself to feel that way. At the same time, she wondered if she really had a chance—did she pick love or did love pick her? Or was she totally naive to confuse a stupid crush with real love? So many questions . . . Where were the answers?

She eventually concluded that she'd been foolish to nurture an interest in someone like Nicholas Prague when it was clear he disliked her. Still, it didn't seem too much to expect for him to be civilized, especially since they were in the same youth group. How was it that all the sweet talk of brotherly love ran rampant on church property but evaporated on school grounds? Just the same, she tried to be polite and friendly to him, but she was rewarded with what felt like cold hostility. Nicholas treated her as if she had cooties. Her respect for him, despite his noble words in youth group and his unbearably good looks, was rapidly deteriorating. In her opinion, Nicholas Prague was a snob. Or worse—a hypocrite.

By the third week of school, Chelsea realized she had an interesting and varied collection of friends. From star quarterback Dayton Moore to academic geek Janelle Parker to ever-adoring Chase Lassiter to chubby but funny Olivia Hutchison. She'd also befriended a couple of drama kids. It wasn't unusual for Chelsea to be surrounded by this diverse gathering of friends during lunch.

She'd also made some frenemies, including popular but snooty Riley Atkins, who sometimes acted nice, as well as the not-so-popular but equally snooty Lishia Vance. Both girls, for whatever reasons, pretended to like Chelsea, but she knew better. Mostly she tried to take girls like that in stride, the same way she took the guys who pursued her in stride.

However, the balancing act, especially with Dayton's constant attentions, was getting more and more difficult.

"You should run for homecoming queen too," Dayton told Chelsea. He pointed up to a glittery poster with Riley's photo beaming down on them. Naturally, Riley had long ago made it clear she intended to win that crown.

"Why would I do that?" Chelsea asked.

"To beat Riley," he said, as if it were obvious.

"You should run," Olivia said from the other end of the lunch table. "I'd help you launch a last-minute campaign."

"So would I," Chase offered. "I could be your campaign manager."

Dayton tossed Chase a warning look.

"Thanks anyway." Chelsea smiled at them. "That's really sweet of you guys, but it's not even a possibility for me. That's the weekend of my dad's wedding, so I won't even be in town."

On their way to drama, Janelle asked Chelsea if she would've run for homecoming queen if her dad's wedding hadn't been a factor.

"You want the truth?"

"Of course," Janelle said.

"I'm so relieved that it's not an option. I'd rather walk over hot coals than run against Riley. That girl hates me."

"How do you know?"

"I can feel it."

"Because of Dayton?"

"I know it makes no sense. According to Dayton, Riley broke up with him. But I have a feeling there's more to the story." She paused by the door to the auditorium.

"There's always more to the story."

As they went backstage, Chelsea asked Janelle how she was enjoying doing makeup. "Are you okay with it?" She lowered her voice. "I know you wanted a part in the play."

"It's only fair. I've gotten so many roles in the past . . . it's my turn to do makeup. And I'm actually getting pretty good at it. I can't wait to try some cherry-red lipstick on you."

Chelsea laughed. "As long as you make me look like Bette Davis, I won't complain."

"I love that we're going with the forties style. So much more dramatic."

"Speaking of dramatic," Mr. Valotti said loudly, "let's get to work, class." He clapped his hands and called them to their places, and they picked up where they'd left off yesterday. There was no place at school where Chelsea felt as comfortable as she did on the stage. Accustomed to acting—wasn't that all she did?—she liked the freedom of stepping into a different character and forgetting all about her own life. In fact, she was getting so comfortable with it that she wasn't even too bothered by Mr. Valotti's "friendliness" toward her. Like so many other things, she was beginning to take it in stride. And when he asked her and a couple of others to stay after school, she didn't feel the least bit concerned.

"I don't like this," Janelle told her as they left the auditorium.

"What?"

Janelle started going on about Mr. Valotti's reputation and how she didn't trust his motives.

"I think he's just the flirty-friendly type," Chelsea said to reassure her. "Like the dogs that are all bark and no bite, he's harmless."

"I think he's lulled you into believing he's harmless."

"Janelle!" Chelsea frowned at her.

"Excuse me for caring about my friend."

Chelsea softened. "I'm glad you care about me, Janelle. So what do you suggest I do?"

Janelle's brow creased. "I'll ask my mom to pick us up, and I'll come with you after school. I'll hang out behind the scenes just to be sure he doesn't try anything untoward."

" 'Untoward'?" Chelsea chuckled. "Only you would use a word like that." She used her hands to measure the height difference between herself and her petite friend. "My personal mini bodyguard. Man, I feel so safe."

"Hey, I might be small, but I have a big set of lungs and I'm not afraid to use them."

Chelsea laughed. "Whatever trips your trigger."

After school, Janelle and Chelsea headed back to the auditorium. As planned, Janelle faded into the scenery and Chelsea waited along the sidelines for her turn to practice her scene. Mr. Valotti finished coaching some of the actors, then excused them. He called up Archer Davis, the guy playing the starring role of the cantankerous Sheridan Whiteside, and Chelsea, who was playing Sheridan's secretary. Mr. Valotti gave them some direction, then told them to begin the scene. After a few do-overs, Mr. Valotti seemed satisfied with Archer's performance.

"That was fine," he told Archer. "Just make sure you work on that pratfall. You need to get it down so that you don't actually break your leg." They laughed, and Mr. Valotti excused Archer, then turned to Chelsea. "I'd like to go over the scene where Maggie meets Bert."

"But Tyler's not here," Chelsea said. Tyler was playing the small-town journalist Bert, Maggie's love interest.

"I'll read his part." Mr. Valotti leaned close to her, reaching across to point at a spot on her script. "Go ahead and start here."

Feeling a bit uneasy but thankful that Janelle was nearby—she was, wasn't she?—Chelsea began to read. It wasn't exactly a steamy scene since Maggie and Bert had only just met. But Mr. Valotti seemed to be taking every opportunity to make it into something more.

"You need to turn up the heat," he told her. "The audience needs to feel the chemistry between Maggie and Bert. You want them to be hooked, anticipating the romance that's coming. So as you read that line, look deeply into Bert's eyes with longing, as if you're seeing the man of your dreams. Can you do that?"

Chelsea swallowed hard. "I think so."

Standing uncomfortably close to her, he read Bert's line, then waited. She took a quick breath and looked directly into Mr. Valotti's eyes. Trying to keep her voice from shaking, she repeated the next line. But her heart was pounding hard, and something about this felt all wrong . . . and scary.

"That was a little bit better, but I think we need to try it—"

"Hey, Chelsea," Janelle called in an offhand way as she came onstage. "Oh, sorry, I didn't realize you were still practicing." She stopped on the sidelines, lowering her voice. "I'll just wait for you here—quiet as a mouse."

Mr. Valotti stepped away from Chelsea and his expression changed. But without missing a beat, he read the next line, and then Chelsea read hers. Following his direction, she continued looking "deeply" into his eyes. But she could tell this was making him uncomfortable now, and for some reason that was satisfying to her. She wanted to make him squirm. Finally he proclaimed practice done, said he'd see them later, and left the stage.

Without speaking, Chelsea tossed Janelle a grateful glance and gathered up her things, and the two of them quickly exited the auditorium. It wasn't until they were safely away from there that Chelsea admitted that Janelle had been right.

"I don't think I was imagining that," she said in a hushed voice. "He was coming on to me. I could feel it. And when you showed up, he acted differently."

"I know." Janelle nodded soberly. "It was freaky to see. I should've popped in sooner, but I was curious as to how far he'd take it."

"Thanks a lot." Chelsea frowned. "I feel like I was your social science experiment."

"Hey, I would've jumped in if I needed to." Janelle sighed. "I think I almost wished he'd stepped over the line. Then we could get him fired."

"That seems a little harsh."

"Really?" Janelle turned and looked intently at Chelsea. "What if he has actually taken it further with other girls? You know what I mean. Would you want to protect him then?"

"No." Chelsea firmly shook her head. "You're right."

"Promise me, Chelsea, if Valotti ever tries anything, you know, *seriously*, that you'll tell on him, okay?"

Chelsea held up her hand like a pledge. "Absolutely. I promise."

"These guys should start a club."

"A club?" Chelsea was confused.

"A jerk club. Guys like Valotti and Dayton and even Chase could all be card-carrying jerks."

"It seems unfair to classify Dayton and Chase in that club," Chelsea said.

"Give them both time, or opportunity, and they'll prove themselves worthy of the title."

"Does that mean you've given up on Chase?" Chelsea asked as they went outside to wait for Janelle's mom.

Janelle gave a loud, exasperated sigh. "When I see Chase drooling over you . . . what am I supposed to do?"

Chelsea studied Janelle as they sat on the steps. As usual of late, Janelle's hair was pulled back in a drab-looking pony-tail, and her face was pretty much devoid of makeup. Even her outfit was kind of ho-hum. Chelsea would never say this out loud, but Janelle seemed to have given up—she seemed content to be dowdy. Unfortunately, she seemed so glum right now that Chelsea didn't have the heart to point this out. But seriously, how did Janelle hope to catch Chase's eye looking like that?

"And you can't exactly lecture me on not giving up on a guy." Janelle gave Chelsea an accusing look.

"What do you mean?" Chelsea knew what she meant, but she hoped if she stalled long enough, Janelle's mom would show up and this conversation would be shelved.

"You know exactly what and who I mean. I still see you looking at Nicholas sometimes—in the exact same way Valotti was trying to get you to look at him."

Chelsea was shocked. "Really? It's that obvious?"

"To me it is. And I'll bet Dayton's noticed it too. Especially since he seems to have taken a real dislike to Nicholas. Have you noticed that?"

"Now that you mention it . . ." Chelsea slowly shook her head as this sank in. "But it's totally ridiculous. Not only does

Nicholas act like I don't exist, he actually seems to despise me. And it's not that I'm into Dayton, but he seriously has nothing to be jealous of when it comes to Nicholas Prague."

"But you wish he did."

Chelsea brushed a piece of lint from her jeans and shrugged.

"I know you do." Janelle lowered her voice, like she thought someone might be listening. "And so does Lishia."

Chelsea blinked. "Lishia likes Nicholas?"

"She's been in love with him for a couple of years now."

"Does he like her?"

"He used to. But that was a long time ago. Like middle school. But she can't seem to get over him."

Chelsea wouldn't admit it, but she could relate.

"Want to know my theory?"

She shrugged. "I guess I might as well since it seems your mother has forgotten us."

"I think Nicholas is afraid of you."

"Huh?"

"You're too pretty, Chelsea."

Chelsea laughed. "Yeah, right. Tell me another one."

Janelle shook her finger at her. "You are! Your stepmom-to-be did too good a job on you. You're the kind of girl who turns heads. Just think of how Valotti was coming on to you, the way Dayton wants to own you body and soul, and how Chase can't keep his eyes off you. That's just to name a few."

"And what does that have to do with Nicholas?"

"I think that, in the same way you attract guys who are jerks, you repel the guys who aren't—at least the ones who are trying not to be jerks."

"That's nuts."

"No, it's not. Think about it. Nicholas recommitted his

life to God. He's trying to make better choices in all areas of his life. Why would he want to risk it all by getting involved with a hot babe like you?"

"That's ridiculous." But even as she said this, Chelsea wasn't so sure.

"No, it isn't. In fact, I heard Nicholas say something to Chase that backs up my theory. He told Chase that if he kept going after the wrong kind of girl, he'd seriously regret it later."

"The *wrong* kind of girl?" Chelsea frowned. "As in me?"

Janelle just nodded.

"Wow, that's pretty judgmental."

"Yeah, it seemed unfair."

Chelsea was trying to grasp this, and she was also trying not to get angry. But it was frustrating—very frustrating! "So what am I supposed to do, Janelle? Do I turn myself back into the drab wallflower I used to be?" She pointed at her friend. "Like you?"

Janelle looked surprised.

"No offense, Janelle, but you have been letting yourself go. I mean, you started out strong at the beginning of school, but then it's like you gave up."

"Gave up?"

"I'm sorry, but it's true. Since you're so good at telling me the truth, I figured I should be able to speak honestly with you. Right?"

Janelle's mom's car pulled up then, but both girls just stared at each other for a long moment. Chelsea knew she'd pushed things too far this time. But how was it fair for Janelle to speak her mind and put down Chelsea, while Chelsea was supposed to keep her opinions to herself?

Still, she regretted her words as they rode home in silence. Mrs. Parker attempted some small talk but finally gave up. Chelsea wished she'd kept her mouth shut. Janelle was the best friend she had—she'd come to Chelsea's rescue with Mr. Valotti. And this was how Chelsea thanked her?

sixteen

Chelsea called Janelle later that night and profusely apologized. "I don't know what came over me or why I said all that," she explained. "I think I was just really frustrated. Please forgive me, Janelle."

"I already did."

"Really?"

"Yeah. God says he forgives us, so in the same way we should forgive others."

"Wow. I guess I should keep that in mind."

"I was actually thinking about the whole thing . . . and I've got an idea."

"An idea?"

"Yeah. You want to come over so we can discuss it?"

"Discuss it?" Chelsea wondered what kind of an idea Janelle could possibly have in mind. "Okay."

Chelsea had been in Janelle's bedroom a few times, but she was still mesmerized by all the old movie posters and theater memorabilia. It was like a drama shrine. Even Janelle's mirror, rimmed with light bulbs, was theatrical looking. It seemed that everywhere Chelsea looked, boas and necklaces and other kinds of costume accessories and props were hanging. Chelsea loved being in this space, and during the time that Lishia had pushed her out, she'd missed it.

"So . . ." Chelsea sat on the edge of Janelle's bed. "What's your big idea?"

Janelle held up a flyer about a youth group camp that was coming up the week after Dad's wedding. "Fall camp."

"Yeah, I know about that."

"I have a plan."

"A plan?"

Janelle began talking about drama and some tricks she'd been learning about theatrical makeup and how it was possible to disguise someone so that they were totally unrecognizable.

"Uh-huh." Chelsea put a hot pink boa around her neck. "And your point is what?"

"We'll make you into a plain Jane."

Chelsea stared at her. "Huh?"

"We'll use a wig and makeup and some drab clothes, maybe even a pair of glasses, and we'll make you into a plain Jane."

Chelsea was still confused. "And why would we want to do that?"

"It'll be a test."

"What kind of a test?"

"To see what Nicholas will do."

"I'm still lost."

"Well, you want to get Nick's attention, right?"

Chelsea shrugged.

"If we transform you into a plain Jane, we can give you a different name and a new identity, and maybe you can get to know him and find out if you two really jive, because he'll have no excuse not to—"

"Yes!" Chelsea stood. "I do get it. Kind of like Eliza Doolittle, only backward. Or sort of." She looked at herself in Janelle's mirror. "But you don't have to make me *ugly*, do you?" She didn't like to think she was shallow, but she wasn't sure she could go back to that . . . not even for a weekend.

"No. Not ugly. Just plain. We'll simply remove the jerk magnet persona." Janelle stepped next to her, then frowned. "We'll make you look more like someone . . . someone like . . . well, like me."

A light went on in Chelsea's head, and she pointed at Janelle's reflection. "And we can make you look more like me!"

"What?"

"Yes!" She turned to face Janelle. "We'll give you the wow factor so that you turn heads, and we'll see if you can catch Chase's attention."

"Oh . . . I don't know." Janelle looked worried.

"Come on, Janelle, if I'm willing to do this, you should be too."

"But what's the point of pretending to be what I'm not to get Chase to look at me?"

"I could say the same to you about me. But this is an experiment, right?"

"Right."

"I'm not doing it unless you're doing it."

Janelle cracked a smile. "It could be pretty hilarious."

"Not to mention revealing."

"I haven't figured out all the details yet."

"But I'm sure you will. And I'll help you."

"I know you have your dad's wedding next weekend. But

that still gives us this weekend to pull something together. Do you really want to do this?"

Chelsea laughed. "Why not?"

They shook hands and immediately began to plan. Janelle would have to get a blonde wig. "At least as long as my hair," Chelsea told her. "And how about wearing some heels to make you seem taller? We don't want your height to give you away."

"Good point." Janelle made some notes. "We have to do everything possible to keep from getting found out."

"That would be so embarrassing."

"And we need to give ourselves new names and new profiles, and we'll need to remember what they are for each other too—unless we want to pretend like we've just met and got stuck in the same room together."

"That might be simpler."

"We can say we're from one of the other schools since there are about six different youth groups that attend fall camp." Janelle pressed her lips together. "I'll try to figure out some way to get us a room to ourselves. Usually there are four to a room . . . but sometimes there are exceptions, like if there's a health concern or some other reason. I'll try to think of a believable excuse."

"Like what?" Chelsea frowned.

"Maybe one of us has a mental issue." Janelle giggled. "Some kind of weird phobia or a snoring disorder or body odor problem. Don't worry, I'll come up with something good and sympathetic too."

Chelsea felt concerned. "Do you think it's wrong to do this?"

"It's an experiment," Janelle assured her. "A social experiment. Who knows, we might be able to use this for school. We could write a paper on it."

Chelsea nodded. "That's true. We probably will make some interesting discoveries." Since Janelle, who'd been going to the church hosting the camp since birth, thought this was okay, Chelsea decided not to question it either. It really could be a very revealing experiment. And who was she to stand in the way of science, or social science, or whatever kind of weird science a crazy plan like this might fall into?

On Saturday they spent the morning going through each of their own closets, coming up with some items that would contribute to some boring plain Jane outfits for Chelsea as well as some more stylish ones for Janelle's new look. Janelle had also borrowed some wigs from the drama department.

"Borrowed?" Chelsea questioned as Janelle worked on the drab brown hair that reminded Chelsea a bit of her previous hair color—muddy and dull.

"Actually, I checked them out," Janelle said. "As part of the hair and makeup crew, I'm allowed to take things home and work on them."

"Oh."

"I'll return them on Monday, then check them out again right before camp."

"Okay . . ."

"Don't worry, no one from drama even goes to our youth group or will be at camp, so no one will have the slightest clue as to what I'm up to." Janelle slipped some glasses with black plastic rims on Chelsea's face.

"Wow, now that really looks different."

"And once I do your makeup—"

"What do you plan to do anyway? Give me warts and a hooked nose?"

"No, silly. You're not supposed to look like the Wicked

Witch of the West." Janelle studied Chelsea closely. "First I'll tone down your complexion so it looks like you don't get much sun, then I'll pale and thin those lips, maybe do something to make your nose a bit less perfect, add a little something to your brow line—"

Chelsea touched her forehead. "You have no idea the pain I went through to get these eyebrows."

"Well, at least this will only be temporary."

"That reminds me of something," Chelsea said. "I told Kate about what we're doing."

"Kate, as in soon-to-be stepmom Kate?"

"Yes. She's my confidante."

"What did she say?"

"She laughed."

Janelle looked relieved.

"And she said if I send her a photo of you, she might have some tips for your makeover."

"My makeover?" Janelle frowned. "Who said anything about a makeover? This is just a theatrical act."

"Fine." Chelsea shrugged. "If you don't want Kate's help, I'll just—"

"No, no," Janelle said quickly. "We should probably take her up on her offer. You can send her my photo."

Using her phone, Chelsea took some pics of Janelle, then sent them to Kate. "By the way, Kate reminded me to ask you if it would be okay for me to kind of stay with you while she and Dad are on their honeymoon."

"Of course. That'll give us even more time to work on this."

"I told Dad I was fine on my own, but he doesn't think I'm old enough."

"Maybe we can use your house to practice our characters

in," Janelle suggested. "I mean, since no one will be around to question us."

"Great idea."

They spent a couple of hours just experimenting with makeup, which was both interesting and scary. Chelsea was surprised at how little it took to change a person back from looking hot to not. She was more than eager to wash off the makeup and go back to her "normal" look. Later in the afternoon, after Janelle's mom took a break from a paper she was working on (she'd returned to school for her master's degree), it was time to do a little shopping.

"Chelsea is helping me with a makeover," Janelle explained to her mom as she drove them to Best 4 Less.

"How nice," Mrs. Parker said with enthusiasm. "Chelsea, we've all noticed that you do have a certain sort of panache style. It would be nice of you to share that with Janelle. Especially since, as everyone knows, I'm not terribly talented at that sort of thing."

"That's probably because you focus more on your mind than your looks," Chelsea said, then regretted her words. "I mean that as a compliment, Mrs. Parker. I think brains are a lot more important than appearances. But I guess it's nice when you can have both."

Janelle told her mom about Chelsea's dad's upcoming marriage and asked if it was okay for Chelsea to stay with them during the honeymoon.

"Of course, we'd love to have you."

"I'll probably be at my house a lot of the time," Chelsea said. "But Dad doesn't want me sleeping there alone."

"Of course not. I'd feel the same about Janelle. How exciting that you're getting a new stepmother."

Janelle told her about how fashionable Kate was and how she'd helped Chelsea with a makeover.

"Kate sounds like a delightful person. You must feel lucky, Chelsea."

"She's pretty cool. Maybe you can get to know her when she moves in with us," Chelsea said. "I know she'll want to make some friends."

At the store, they first looked for some stylish pieces for Janelle. Chelsea could tell she was pushing her friend way beyond her comfort zone, but wasn't that what this was about? After they'd found some perfect items, they went over to the bargain rack to look for some plain Jane pieces for Chelsea.

"You're a natural at finding the most practical and boring kinds of clothes," Chelsea told her as Janelle held up a dull beige sweater for Chelsea to preview in the mirror. "Even with makeup on, this color makes my face look like death warmed over."

Janelle laughed. "Perfect."

"These are just the kinds of things that Kate told me to avoid."

"See, I'm really good at this."

They'd just gone into the changing area again when Chelsea got a text from Kate. "She's got some suggestions," Chelsea said from her fitting room.

"Such as?" Janelle was right next to her.

"She agrees with my hair direction. She also says you need to get your eyebrows done professionally. She's going to re-search some recommendations for you."

"But that's permanent."

Chelsea thought about this. "Yes, but you'll probably like

it. You can make an appointment for right after school on Friday so no one sees it before camp."

"Okay."

"And there are some other things. Do you want me to text her back with the green light to go ahead and make your appointments if she finds some places?"

"I guess so. But it'll all have to be that Friday afternoon."

"I'll let her know."

Finally, with their purchases made, they were riding back home with Chelsea's dad. "Did you girls have fun shopping?" he asked.

They both chimed out a yes.

"Hopefully it didn't set me back too much."

"I actually shopped the clearance rack," Chelsea told him.

"Really?" He sounded slightly concerned. "Hopefully Kate won't think she failed you."

Chelsea laughed. "Just some casual clothes for camp," she said. "Don't worry."

"And that camp happens while Kate and I are still in Hawaii?"

"That's right."

"But you'll make sure I have all the phone numbers and info, right?"

"Yes, Dad." She rolled her eyes at Janelle.

"Well, you have to admit that it's a little odd for a father to be leaving his daughter home alone while he goes on his honeymoon."

"Would you rather take me along with you?"

He chuckled. "No, probably not."

"We'll keep a good eye on her," Janelle assured him.

"I appreciate that." He sighed. "I can't believe the big day is just one week away."

The next week passed in a kind of blur. Between school, drama responsibilities, Dayton's pressures to commit to a serious dating relationship, preparing for their camp charade, and getting ready for the wedding, Chelsea felt slightly dizzy by Thursday.

"I can't believe you're missing homecoming this weekend," Dayton said for what seemed like the hundredth time. "Who will I dance with on Saturday night?"

Chelsea nodded over to where Riley was sitting with her group of friends. "I can think of a few options."

"You really want me to do that to you?" Dayton demanded.

She shrugged. "Like I keep telling you, Dayton, I really don't want to get serious. You're wasting your time on me."

He looked disappointed.

"If you want to step aside, there are others who would gladly step in," Chase said to Dayton.

Dayton gave him a smoldering look.

"Just kidding, man." Chase held up his hands.

"By the way," Chelsea said, "good luck at the game tomorrow night."

"Why are you telling me that now?" Dayton asked.

"Remember? Dad and I are flying out tonight. I won't be at school tomorrow."

He shook his head. "Running out on me in my hour of need."

She smiled sympathetically and patted his hand. As she did, she caught Nicholas giving her a disapproving look. "You'll do fine without me for a few days."

"Hey." Chase pulled one of the fall camp flyers from his pocket. "I almost forgot. Tomorrow's the deadline for fall camp, Chelsea. Are you signed up yet?"

Chelsea glanced at Janelle.

"As a matter of fact, Chelsea isn't going," Janelle told him. "And neither am I."

"Why not?" Chase frowned.

"We have other plans," Janelle said nonchalantly.

"But it's a great camp." He turned to Chelsea. "It's the coolest place, down by Monterey."

"Sorry." Chelsea held up her hands helplessly.

"We already promised to spend the weekend with my aunt in San Francisco," Janelle said. "She's taking us to a musical on Saturday, and then we'll do shopping and eat at some cool restaurants . . . lots of fun stuff."

"And I've never seen San Francisco," Chelsea said. At least that was true.

"But camp is fun," Chase said a bit meekly.

Dayton laughed. "Let's see, if I had to choose between church camp and a weekend in San Francisco . . . hmm, I don't know . . ."

"It *will* be fun," Lishia insisted. "I'm going."

"If you say so," Dayton said in a teasing tone.

"It probably would be fun," Chelsea said quickly. "Maybe next year."

"Come on, Chelsea." Dayton grabbed her by the hand. "Something I want to show you."

"But I'm not done with—"

"Oh, come on. It'll only take a few minutes."

Chelsea didn't want to go, but she didn't want to make a fuss. She allowed Dayton to pull her away, but as they were leaving she noticed that Nicholas was still watching . . . and frowning.

As it turned out, Dayton wanted to show her the trophy

case where they'd just put the photo of this year's football team. At least that was what he said he wanted to show her. But once they were there, hidden in the shadowy part of the hallway, he pulled her close to him. "Oh, Chelsea," he said, his breath coming directly into her face, "can't you see how crazy you're making me?"

"Crazy?" His grip felt tight on her arms, so tight it almost hurt.

"Stringing me along like this, playing hard to get . . . Can't you see it just makes me want you even more?" He moved closer to her. "Please, Chelsea, give me a break," he whispered. "I want you, girl, more than I've ever wanted anything." He leaned toward her like he was about to kiss her, but she turned her head and his lips brushed her cheek.

"Please, Dayton," she whispered back, "you're hurting my arms."

"Fine." He let her go and she nearly fell backward. "But don't expect me to keep waiting for you!"

"I don't, Dayton." She looked directly into his eyes. "I've told you from the start that I could only offer you my friendship."

His face darkened with anger, then he swore and stormed away. For a moment she felt terrible, like she really was guilty of leading him on, but then she just felt relieved. At least now it would be over.

"Looks like I was right."

Chelsea turned to see Janelle, her arms folded across her front. "Right about what?"

"Dayton. He turned out to be a jerk, right?"

Chelsea shrugged. "Did you follow us here?"

Janelle shrugged. "Some of your friends were worried."

"Worried?"

"You know, that Dayton was dragging you off to have his way with you."

Chelsea laughed. "And they sent Baby Face to defend my honor?"

Janelle laughed too. "I guess so."

As Chelsea waited for Dad to pick her up after school, she couldn't help but wonder if Janelle or the others had had reason to be worried when Dayton pulled his macho He-Man routine. What if she had been somewhere with no one else around? The truth was she had felt frightened by him. His anger and frustration had been palpable. Even now, her arms hurt from how hard he'd squeezed, and she suspected he'd left marks. She wondered if he'd ever pulled something like that on Riley. If so, was that why Riley had broken up with him?

Too many questions . . . not enough answers.

Fortunately, Dad arrived, and before long they were so focused on catching their flight and the wedding plans and practicing "Do You Know the Way to San Jose?" and so many other things that she soon forgot about poor Dayton and his unrealistic demands. A few days away from him and everyone and everything else in San Jose would be welcome!

seventeen

There was something refreshing about being with adults again. It was odd, since for so many years Chelsea had totally resented the way she was always stuck in grown-up social situations instead of spending time with her own peers. Of course, that had simply been one of the many consequences of being a wallflower. But it felt familiar and comfortable now.

Being around Dad and Kate and their friends on Friday, going to the bridal shower that evening and a bridesmaid breakfast on Saturday morning—well, it all felt kind of relaxed and easy and fun. Quite a contrast to what Chelsea had been through recently, with her attempts to adjust to her new image, new friends, and a new school. Compared to that, this was a piece of cake—wedding cake.

The wedding ceremony was small and intimate. The chapel with stained-glass windows, the violin and cello, white roses, and creamy white satin—very romantic. So much so that Chelsea imagined that she might someday want a wedding similar to this one. Seeing Dad and Kate standing before the minister with tears in their eyes as they exchanged vows and rings made Chelsea cry too. It was sweet and wonderful, and she was happy for them.

The reception, held in a downtown hotel ballroom, was larger than the wedding and more lively and fun. Chelsea, still pretending she was an adult, enjoyed dancing with some of the guests and drinking her faux champagne as they toasted the newlyweds.

Before the party ended, Dad and Chelsea, with the background music of a borrowed karaoke CD, sang "Do You Know the Way to San Jose?" Everyone laughed and clapped, and Kate hugged them both. "That was absolutely beautiful!" She kissed Chelsea on both cheeks. "Thank you so much, darling. Thank you for allowing me into your life. And thank you for sharing your dad with me."

Chelsea was crying again. "Thank you too, Kate. I'm so glad you're part of our family now. I really need you in my life."

Dad hugged and kissed her, saying all the things he probably thought she wanted to hear, like she was still his number one girl and that sort of fatherly thing. But she forgave him for it. She knew his heart was in the right place. She also knew that, as much as she loved Kate and Dad and wanted the best for them, she was no longer Dad's number one girl. That was impossible.

Finally the happy couple told everyone goodbye and departed for their honeymoon. The plan was for them to ride the limo to the airport, where they would board an all-night flight that would land them, pleasantly exhausted, in Maui early in the morning tomorrow. Meanwhile Chelsea would go home with Kate's mom, Margie, where she would spend the night. Tomorrow morning, Margie would deliver Chelsea to the airport to catch a flight back to San Jose, where Janelle and her mom had promised to pick up Chelsea around noon.

Chelsea knew she should be delighted that all the wedding festivities had gone so smoothly—they were hitched without a hitch. Right now she should be relieved that Dad and Kate were on their flight and safely on their way. Yet she felt inexplicably sad and lonely as she climbed into the squeaky bed in Margie's musty-smelling guest room that night.

Chelsea closed her eyes and knew that, without God to talk to right now, she probably would be crying herself to sleep. As it was, she still felt a large, hard lump in her throat, and keeping the tears at bay was a challenge. So she prayed for strength.

On the way home from the airport, Janelle filled Chelsea in on the latest happenings at their school. Riley Atkins had lost the homecoming queen crown to one of her best friends. "Although I'm sure Vanessa Renaldo can consider herself an ex-friend now. No one even knows how she won since Vanessa is even snootier than Riley."

"I feel sorry for Riley," Chelsea said.

"So do I," Mrs. Parker said.

Janelle rolled her eyes.

To change the subject and to fill in the empty air, Chelsea told them about the wedding, yapping on and on until they were home. "I'm going to go to my house for a while," she said, "just to do homework and stuff."

"Feel free to come over whenever you like," Mrs. Parker said. "Dinner's at seven."

"You don't really have to come to dinner unless you want to," Janelle told her as she and Chelsea walked next door. "I wouldn't if I were you."

"I think dinner with a family sounds fun."

Again Janelle rolled her eyes. Then she told Chelsea about her latest plans for camp next weekend. "I got us a room to ourselves."

"How?"

"Promise you won't get mad?"

"What did you do?" Chelsea paused from unlocking the front door.

"I called and told the registrar that you had AIDS."

"AIDS?"

"She promised to keep it hush-hush."

"AIDS?"

"Actually, I said HIV. I said it was the result of a blood transfusion during your appendectomy."

"My *appendectomy?*" Chelsea suppressed the urge to scream as she went into the living room and dumped her bags.

"When you were six," Janelle explained like she was reading a medical report, "your appendix nearly burst. They got it out just in time, but because you were in a third-world country, the blood was infected with—"

"Third-world country?" Chelsea stared at Janelle.

"Uganda. Your parents were missionaries. They had to come home due to your health issues."

"You should start writing novels."

"Anyway, I told the registrar that you were very self-conscious about the whole thing, and it was hard enough to get you to come to camp without you feeling like everyone knows this about you."

"Right." Chelsea sank down on the sofa and just shook her head. "I leave you alone for a few days, and this is what happens."

"Hey, it's not easy to get a room to ourselves."

"Janelle . . ." Chelsea sighed. "Maybe this isn't such a good idea."

"It's a great idea. And it's going to be my research project—I'm going to use it for my psychology class. Also, I plan to keep those appointments at the places Kate called for me. I'm actually starting to look forward to this."

"Really? You mean the makeover part or camp?"

"Both."

Chelsea didn't know what to say. On the flight home, she'd decided to pull the plug on this plan, but seeing Janelle so gung ho made it difficult. "Well, I need to do some laundry." She stood and picked up her bags. "And I've got homework to do."

"I emailed you some homework too." Janelle stood and smiled. "I'm glad you're home, Chelsea. I missed you."

Chelsea hugged her. "Thanks. I missed you too."

Janelle went back to her house, and Chelsea got her first load of laundry going and started to work on her homework. Her plan now was to put fall camp out of her mind. After all, she had all week to figure that one out. But homework was due tomorrow. First things first.

eighteen

To Chelsea's disappointment, Dayton apologized to her on Monday. Taking her aside in the cafeteria, he told her he was sincerely sorry. "I don't know what came over me," he finally said. "I think I was just all worked up over the game and homecoming and stuff."

"Dayton," she began carefully, "I accept your apology. But I have to stick to what I already told you. I only want to be friends."

He frowned. "I blew it, didn't I?"

"No." She shook her head. "What you did last week didn't change anything with me. It is what it is, Dayton. You've been a good friend, and I'd really like to keep it that way."

Chelsea noticed a number of people watching them. Some furtively. Some, like Riley, were blatantly staring.

His face got stony, like he couldn't believe she was turning him down again.

"Dayton?"

"What?"

"What happened between you and Riley?"

He shook his head. "I told you already. We broke up."

"You said she broke up with you, right?"

"She did."

"Why?"

"Huh?" He looked confused.

"Why did she break up with you? I mean, I see her watching you and me all the time. She's not going with anyone else. I'm just curious . . . why did she break up with you when it seems like she still likes you?"

He shrugged. "What's the difference?"

"I'm just curious."

"Then maybe you should ask her." He shoved his hands in his pockets.

She put a hand on his shoulder. "I do mean it though, Dayton. I would still like to be your friend. But I'll understand if you don't want that."

Again he shook his head, then he turned and walked away. Suddenly she felt even more conspicuous. Standing there by herself, she wasn't sure whether she should walk away too. Or maybe she should return to where Janelle and some of the others were sitting. Finally she decided to do something totally out of the blue. No one, not even Dayton, would expect her to do this.

She walked over to Riley. "Can we talk?" she asked.

Riley looked surprised, understandably. But she stood and followed Chelsea over to an empty table by the wall, where they both sat down. "I don't know if you know it or not, but I've never really been dating Dayton. We've only been friends. That's all."

Riley's expression was blank. "I don't know why that should concern me one way or another."

"I don't know either." Chelsea studied her closely. "Except that I always catch you watching me when I'm with Dayton, and you've seemed, uh, unhappy about it."

Riley's expression crumbled a bit, and she looked uneasy.

"I get the impression that you might still like him."

"That's totally ridiculous."

"Really?"

Riley's blue eyes flashed. "Did he tell you that?"

"No. Not at all. In fact, he wouldn't even tell me why you guys broke up in the first place."

"Maybe it's none of your business." Riley gave her a hard look, flipping her shiny blonde hair over her shoulder almost like a challenge.

"Maybe." For a brief instant Chelsea felt in over her head. What was she doing sitting here talking about all this with someone like Riley? Just the same, she continued. "Do you want to know what I think?"

Riley gave a half shrug.

"Fine, I won't bore you with it then." Chelsea stood.

"Wait." Riley looked at her with desperation. "Yes, I'd like to hear what you think. Please, sit down."

Chelsea sat back down. "Okay." She took a deep breath. "I think Dayton still likes you, Riley, and I think you still like him. But I think he hurt your feelings last year. I suspect he pressured you, just like he's pressured me from time to time, and I think you'd had enough. Is that about right?"

Riley sighed, then nodded.

"Maybe you did the right thing too, I mean by breaking up." Chelsea drummed her fingers on the table. "Dayton does need to be put in his place sometimes. He can be too pushy and demanding."

"That's for sure."

"I'm not suggesting you give him a second chance . . ."

Riley locked eyes with her. "What then?"

Chelsea shrugged. "I'm not sure. I guess I'm saying I understand."

Riley's expression softened. "Thanks."

"But if you do get back with him . . . stand your ground. Don't let him push you around. Okay?"

Riley smiled. "Yeah. I get you."

"Sorry to hear you lost homecoming queen last week."

Riley's mouth twisted slightly to one side. "It wasn't a big deal."

Feeling there was nothing left to say, Chelsea started to leave.

"Wait, Chelsea."

She paused.

"Why did you bother to tell me any of that? I mean, you didn't have to. I certainly haven't been very nice to you."

"I think it's because on one level I do like Dayton. I think he could be an okay guy. But he needs to stop acting like a jerk."

Riley laughed. "You got that right!"

Chelsea smiled. "I'm sure that you, like me, get tired of attracting guys who are jerks. I mean, who needs a jerk by her side?"

"For sure." Riley lifted a hand to give her a high five.

Chelsea slapped her palm. "But maybe there's hope for Dayton. Like maybe the right girl—a strong one who really cares about him—might be able to reform the poor guy."

Riley nodded. "Dayton as a reformed jerk. I can imagine that."

"You'd have your work cut out for you."

"It might be worth one more shot."

Chelsea shrugged. "So I guess that's why I told you." Chelsea saw that even more eyes were watching her now. Because she didn't want to have to go back to her friends and explain the whole thing in detail, like they would want, she just wished Riley good luck and exited the cafeteria. Maybe she would keep them guessing.

For the rest of the week, Chelsea and Janelle practiced their characters every evening. Chelsea became Trina Johnson, a mousy, geeky, shy girl. Janelle turned herself into Brittany Woodard, a pretty, witty blonde whose family had recently relocated from Mobile, Alabama.

"I watch *Sweet Home Alabama* every night before I go to bed," she confessed. "I actually woke up with a Southern drawl this morning, and I had to remember to switch back to my normal voice at school."

Doing the Trina character was frighteningly easy for Chelsea. Other than a change in her voice, which she lowered to avoid being recognized, Trina's demeanor and mannerisms were nearly identical to the old Chelsea. So much so that as Friday approached, Chelsea/Trina no longer felt guilty about the little experiment they were conducting. She was simply playing her previous self by another name.

Janelle had done a good job of developing her character too. Between her Southern drawl, which she had down pat, and her flamboyant gestures, she could pass as Reese Witherspoon's little sister.

"Just be careful not to go too far with the Southern lingo,"

Chelsea told her Thursday night. "You don't want to come across as a cartoon character."

"You think I look like a cartoon?" Janelle peered at herself in the mirror, patting her very realistic-looking wig—she'd spent hours working on that wig to get it just right. It was amazing how much it changed Janelle to go from brunette to blonde.

"You look fantastic," Chelsea reassured her. "I was talking about how you sound. Don't get too goofy or people will start to wonder. I really want to pull this off."

"Wait until you see me in *full* costume." Janelle practiced her strut, going back and forth from the kitchen to the great room in Chelsea's house. It had been a challenge for her to get used to the platform boots she'd gotten for her role, but those boots combined with the straight-legged jeans really did make her look taller.

Chelsea pointed to Janelle's fuller-than-usual chest. "I thought you were in full costume."

Janelle laughed. "Well, as far as clothing goes. But I still have my appointment tomorrow, which reminds me—I told Mom that you and I were going to be in a camp skit and that we had to go in costume."

"Huh?"

"You should be glad that I was partially telling the truth," Janelle said. "I told her we were doing a role reversal skit to show kids how they sometimes treat people differently just because they look differently, and how that can be hurtful. My mom actually thought it was a cool idea. She promised not to tell anyone."

"But what if someone sees her dropping us off at church? Won't they recognize your car and your mom and figure it out?" Chelsea hadn't really thought about all these details until now.

"My mom will be dropping us off at a different church—it's a really big one in the city, the one I registered us with. I told Mom we need to go there so that our youth group wouldn't catch on to our disguise and spill the beans."

"Man, Janelle, with a mind like yours, I hope you never decide to go into a life of crime."

Janelle laughed as she adjusted the belt she'd borrowed from Chelsea, which looked great on her jeans. "Don't worry. I have no desire to spend time behind bars."

"What do you think will happen if we get caught doing this?"

"Believe me, I've given that a lot of thought. And I decided we'll simply tell the truth—because we *are* doing a social experiment. Really, why should anyone care? The worst they could do would be to send us home, and I kind of doubt that would happen. I mean, once they understood our reasoning."

Chelsea nodded. "That's true."

"So don't worry, okay?"

"Okay."

Thanks to Janelle's detail-oriented planning, everything went smoothly on Friday afternoon, and by six o'clock they were settled into their room at the coastal camp retreat.

"You look so hot," Chelsea told Janelle as she watched her friend touching up her makeup. "No one will know who you are."

Janelle frowned. "Meaning I was so not hot before?"

Chelsea chuckled. "Well, you gotta admit you didn't look like this."

Janelle smoothed her sleek blonde tresses. "I was actually considering changing my real hair color. What do you think?"

Chelsea grimaced. "I, uh, I don't know. I mean, your natural hair color is nice."

Janelle pouted. "But you changed yours."

"That's true, but my original hair color was really mousy." She pointed to her wig. "Even worse than this."

"Worse than that?" Janelle looked surprised. "Wow, I can see why you changed it." She smiled. "Don't you love how geeky those glasses make you look?"

"I thought they made me look smarter."

"In a geeky sort of way. I'm glad we didn't go with the more stylish frames. You might've actually looked good." She reached for a tube of beige waterproof makeup. "Try this to tone down your lips some more." She frowned. "You really have a nice mouth, Chelsea. It's hard to make it look bad."

"Thanks. But the name is Trina, remember."

"Oh, yeah. In fact, that gives me an idea, *Trina*."

"What's that?" Chelsea smudged her lips, making them look pathetically pale, about the same color as her pasty face, and almost sickly.

"Let's try to stay in character even when we're alone, okay?"

"Okay."

"Ready to rock and roll?" Janelle/Brittany was strutting across the room like a rock star, and looking so hot that Chelsea/Trina felt more than a little jealous.

"I . . . uh . . . I guess so." Already Chelsea/Trina felt so insecure that she wondered if she had actually unraveled all the self-confidence she'd worked so hard to create for herself over the summer.

As they walked to the dining hall, Chelsea knew they made an unlikely pair, but probably not that much different than they were in their previous personas—just reversed. Except the height difference between them was decreased thanks to Chelsea's flat shoes and flat hair, which made her seem shorter than usual, and Janelle's high heels and fluffy hair, which added to her height.

Already a lot of teens were milling about the dining hall, small clusters and cliques from various youth groups, casting furtive glances at whoever walked in. As planned, Janelle took the lead, cheerfully introducing herself to a couple of guys standing by the door. She told them she was a newcomer to the area, saying how her dad's job was transferred from Mobile and they'd only been to church a couple of times.

"So I don't know a living soul here, and I feel like a fish outta water." She introduced her friend Trina. "I had to twist poor Trina's arm half off to get her to come to this camp with me," Janelle drawled, "so I do hope y'all will make her feel warm and welcome too." When questioned about school, she told them that she and Trina attended a private school, using a phony name so no one could question it. Chelsea just nodded shyly, ducking her head from time to time and acting as awkward as she felt. It actually felt frighteningly natural. Spying Chase coming through the doorway, she gently elbowed Janelle.

"So tell me, does everyone already know everyone here?" She smiled prettily. "I mean, are y'all friends?"

"We know some of the kids here," a guy named Kenneth told her. "But not everyone. We come from several different schools." Already Kenneth seemed hooked by Janelle's Southern charm. "But by Sunday we'll know a lot more people. It's pretty cool how that works."

"How about those boys over there?" Janelle nodded to Chase and Nicholas. "Do they go to your school too?"

"No," Kenneth told them. "But I know Nicholas from summer camp. He's a really great guy. Hey, Nick!" He waved Nicholas over and introduced him to Brittany Woodard. Then he peered at Chelsea. "I'm sorry, I forgot your name."

"It's okay," Chelsea mumbled. "Everyone does."

"Her name is Trina Johnson," Janelle announced, "and she's just about the sweetest friend a girl could have." She stuck her lower lip out in a pout as she linked her arm in Chelsea's. "In fact, she's the only friend I have. I just don't understand the girls up here—they can be so mean."

"Where are you from?" Chase asked Janelle.

"Mobile, Alabama," she told him. "I'm sorry, I don't believe I caught your name."

Chase was introduced, and taking advantage of "Brittany's" attention directed toward him, he peppered her with questions. Without missing a beat, she answered him with even more Southern wit and charm. Janelle really had it going on, and Chelsea could almost imagine those boys eating out of her hand. She was truly the belle of the ball.

Meanwhile, Chelsea/Trina wanted to blend into the woodwork as she folded her arms tightly across her front and stepped away from the throng of kids, mostly guys, who were flocking around Janelle. She wished she could make an adjustment to the straitjacket bra that Janelle had insisted she wear. More than that, she wished this weekend was over. Tugging on the cuff of her frumpy beige sweater, she wondered why she'd ever agreed to this crazy experiment. It wasn't as if she needed to be reminded of what her former life was like.

Nicholas came over to stand with her. "So, Trina, have you ever been to a church camp before?"

Surprised at his attention, Chelsea looked directly at him, then down again as she shook her head. "No. This is all new to me." That was true.

"And you go to private school with Brittany?"

"That's right." She looked back up at him, wondering if he suspected something, but his expression seemed genuine.

"Well, I hope you'll feel welcome here."

"Everyone seems very nice," she told him.

"It's a good group of kids. We're not perfect by any means. But most of us are trying to live our lives for God, or at least we're here to find out more about him."

"Is that what this camp is for?" she asked. "To find out more about God?"

"Yes. Didn't you know that?"

"Not really. But that sounds good to me."

He looked surprised. "So you want to find out more about God?"

"I do." She nodded. "I really do."

He asked if she wanted to talk to him about her experience with God, and for a moment Chelsea forgot she was playing a role. She admitted that she really did want to talk about it. "I recently made a commitment," she said. "No one besides . . . Brittany knows about it." She glanced over to where Janelle/Brittany was still entertaining a small crowd, almost like she was on stage.

"I'd be happy to—" He was cut off by an air horn.

"Okay, campers, it looks like dinner is ready to be served," a guy from up front announced. "Let's start finding our seats and get on with it."

"Come on," Nicholas told her. "You can sit with me."

Chelsea blinked. "Uh, okay." She looked over to where Chase seemed to be leading Janelle/Brittany toward them. Just like that they were seated together, along with Olivia and a couple of others from their church's youth group. The banter was familiar, but instead of attempting to get involved like she normally would, Chelsea just stared down at her white paper placemat and wished she could disappear into thin air. As badly as she'd wanted to get to know Nicholas—before, anyway—she had no desire to do it like this. It was a terrible plan, and she knew she would regret it even more as the weekend progressed. Perhaps she'd spend the weekend in her room. After all, wasn't she supposed to be sickly?

The blessing was said, and food servers came out and began to set dishes of food in front of them. Chelsea's stomach was tied in knots, and she wasn't sure she'd be able to eat. She remembered how Kate used to coach her in an effort to calm her nerves—slow and easy. She picked up her fork and slipped it into the spaghetti, turning it around and around and around as the kids at her table continued to talk and laugh and tease and joke. She couldn't remember when she'd ever felt more out of place, more like an oddity, more like a loser, than right now.

As she attempted to eat, Nicholas worked hard to make small talk with her. She tried to sound responsive and interested, but it was the hardest thing she'd ever done. Not only did she feel like a misfit, she felt like a phony.

"Where are Chelsea and Janelle?" asked Sam, one of the

youth group guys. He went to another school and obviously hadn't heard. "Aren't those two coming?"

"They're off in San Francisco," Lishia told him.

"Too bad." Sam shook his head. "I was hoping to spend some time with Chelsea."

Chase playfully slugged Sam in the arm. "She probably wasn't hoping to spend time with you."

"Why not?" Sam retorted. "She seems like a pretty nice girl to me."

"Don't you mean she seems like a pretty *hot* girl?" Chase challenged.

"I heard she broke up with Dayton last week," someone said.

"Yeah, we saw the whole thing," Olivia told them. She gave her eyewitness report, which was mostly inaccurate. Not that Chelsea planned to straighten them out. It was all she could do to keep from looking at Janelle, which she knew wouldn't be smart right now.

"Well, if Chelsea is really a Christian," Lishia said, "I don't see why she was going with someone like Dayton Moore in the first place. A Christian girl wouldn't do that."

"Who said she's a Christian?" Nicholas said. "Maybe you're wrong to judge her by Christian standards."

"Who is this Chelsea person anyway?" Janelle asked Chase, "and why is she such a hot topic?"

"Chelsea's part of our youth group," Chase explained. "And she's a hot topic because she's a hot girl." He grinned at Janelle. "But not as hot as you."

Janelle actually batted her eyelashes—rather, her fake eyelashes. "Thank you, Chase. You're so sweet I'll bet sugar won't even melt in your mouth."

He didn't seem to know how to respond to that. But unfortunately, the topic remained on Chelsea. While it was slightly amusing to think that she was so interesting to them, it was also irksome and hurtful to hear their candid opinions of her. Finally she couldn't take it anymore.

"I'm sorry," she said as she stood, "but I didn't know Christians liked to gossip so much. Please excuse me." She walked out of the dining room and back to her room, where she was determined to stay until Sunday.

It wasn't long until her cell phone rang. "Trina?" Janelle's voice rang out. "Are you all right, darling?"

"I'm fine," Chelsea told her. "I just needed a break from the catty Christians."

"I understand completely," Janelle drawled. "I'm only calling to tell you that there will be a group meeting at eight—"

"Thanks but no thanks."

"All right then, darling. I'll see you later."

"Have fun." And Chelsea meant it. At least one of them should be having fun with this experiment. Perhaps by tomorrow, Chelsea would feel like having fun too. She was about to turn off her cell phone when she noticed that Dad had called, and she decided to call him back. Kate answered, and Chelsea asked how they were doing.

"Maui is beautiful and wonderful," Kate told her, "but I think both your dad and I are ready to come home."

"Well, you only have a couple more days," Chelsea reminded her. "I wish I were there." She filled Kate in on how their little experiment was going, although she tried to keep it upbeat.

Kate laughed. "I think that sounds like fun."

Chelsea sighed. "I'll admit it's an eye-opener. And Janelle

is sure enjoying herself." She thanked Kate for helping Janelle with her makeover. "She actually looks pretty hot, even without the blonde wig." Suddenly Chelsea heard someone knocking at the door. "I'll bet that's her now," she said. "She probably forgot her key." They said goodbye, and Chelsea went to open the door. Seeing it wasn't Janelle but Nicholas, she opened the door to about a two-inch crack. Trying to act embarrassed that he'd come to their room, she was actually trying to cover up the curious-looking clutter in their *dressing room*.

"Sorry to bother you," Nicholas said. "But I was hoping we could talk."

"Oh . . . I don't know."

"Want to come out and get a soda or something?"

Despite herself, she felt caught up again. On so many levels, Nicholas seemed like a great guy. "Okay. Give me a minute." Thankful she hadn't ripped off the wig like she'd meant to do, she closed the door and ran over to check herself in the mirror. She touched up her lips, smoothed her boring brown bob, and put her glasses back on, then took in a deep, steadying breath. Maybe she could do this.

nineteen

First of all, I want to apologize," Nicholas told Chelsea as they walked down a stone path. "Like I said earlier, just because we're Christians doesn't mean we're perfect. Far from it. The main difference between Christians and everyone else is that Christians know that God has forgiven them for their blunders. Unfortunately, like you witnessed tonight, we still blunder."

"Oh."

He talked a bit more about how he and other Christians were works in progress. "Anytime a Christian thinks he's arrived, he better watch out. I know from experience that we can fall on our faces just like that." He stopped in front of the camp café, asked her what she wanted, then went inside to order them sodas. She nervously waited outside at a little table, wondering what to do.

"Here you go," he said as he set the paper cups on the table and sat down. "I'm really sorry, Trina," he said again, "that your first camp experience started out on such a sour note."

She shrugged. "It's okay . . . but it does make me wonder."

"About what?"

"That girl everyone was talking about." Chelsea looked down at her drink. "I'm curious why they were so down on her. Did she do something to offend them or something?"

He laughed. "No, I don't think so. Between you and me, I think the problem with Chelsea is that she's too pretty for her own good."

"What?" Chelsea peered through her glasses at him. "How is that possible?"

"I'm sure it sounds bizarre, but I think it's true."

"Why do you say that?"

"Girls like that . . . well, it seems like they might care more about the outside than the inside."

"So you know this girl fairly well?" Chelsea was feeling bolder now. "You've spent a lot of time with her?"

"Not really. But I know about those kinds of girls."

"You mean the ones who are too pretty?"

He nodded.

"Would you put my friend Brittany in that category?"

He looked caught off guard. "I didn't mean to suggest that. She seems very sweet."

"But too pretty?"

"Maybe . . . I've warned Chase to steer clear of girls like that. Not that it does much good. Seriously, he seems determined to, well, you know, get a hot girlfriend."

"And you'd never do that yourself? I mean, get a hot girlfriend?"

"No way." He looked intently at her. "That's like asking for trouble."

"Why is that, exactly?"

He smiled at her. "It's just that girls like that—the ones

who are so focused on their hair and their clothes and all that other outward stuff—tend to be shallow."

"Have you known quite a few girls like that?"

"To be honest, only a few. But I picked up on the pattern after about the third one. Then I recommitted my heart to God and realized that I need to avoid girls like that. It might sound extreme, but they're like poison to me."

"So is that how you treat that girl—what was her name?"

"Chelsea? Yeah, I guess I do." He frowned. "That probably sounds all wrong though."

"It seems a little cruel. What if Chelsea wasn't the person you assumed she was? What if all this time you were treating her like poison, and she turned out to be just another ordinary girl, except that she had a pretty veneer, and you never even gave her a chance?"

"When you put it that way, it does seem a little harsh."

She pointed at him. "What if people, particularly girls, treated you like that?"

"What?"

"You know, like if they held you at arm's length because you were too good-looking. How would that make you feel?"

"I'm not sure."

"Would you feel unfairly judged?"

He seemed to be considering this.

"What if I stood up right now and said, 'Nicholas, you are just too handsome for me to be talking to you. So why don't you go take a hike?'"

He gave an uncomfortable smile. "I guess I might feel a little hurt by that."

"Is that the way Christians are supposed to treat each other? Make judgments like that? Keep each other at a distance?"

He frowned. "You're making some good points, Trina."

"Well, being a Christian is still new to me. I'd like to figure some of these things out. To be honest, some of the things I'm experiencing feel a little confusing."

"Probably because, like I said, Christians aren't perfect."

"But some of them act like they are. Or maybe it's just that some of them act like they're superior to others." She studied him.

"That's a fair observation." He pressed his lips together. "I'm sure I act like that sometimes."

"Why?" she demanded.

He looked thoughtful. "That's a really good question, Trina. I think it's kind of a balancing act. You know . . . like, as a Christian, I realize I belong to God. I've been adopted into his family. That makes me feel special. And maybe I lose sight of the fact that I'm a sinner just like everyone else. Maybe I get a little smug."

She just nodded.

"I really like talking to you," he said suddenly. "You're making me think about some things in a new way. And it's good." He glanced at his watch as he stood. "But it's about time for the meeting now. Are you going to come?"

"I don't know." She sighed. "Earlier I'd decided to spend the weekend in my room."

"Please don't do that." He reached for her hand. "Come on, Trina. Come to the meeting. I think you'll enjoy it."

"Okay." She stood. He was still holding her hand.

"We better hurry."

To her surprise, he continued to hold her hand, swinging it as they walked. Her emotions were a wild mixture of guilt and pleasure, anxiety and hope.

"I talked Trina into coming back," he announced to Chase and some of the others. "I hope we can all try harder to make her welcome here." He smiled at Janelle. "And you too, Brittany."

Nicholas sat down next to Chelsea, and she continued to feel a bunch of contrasting emotions. Part of her said to just go with it. Another part of her felt more like a hypocrite than ever. But she didn't have long to think about these things because the band started to play, and the next thing she knew, they were all standing, singing, and clapping.

By mid-afternoon on Saturday, both Janelle and Chelsea were thoroughly sick of their charade. Taking a break in their room, Janelle had her tired feet propped up on the bed. "I'll admit it's been a good lesson in human nature," she said as she typed something into her laptop. She really was taking the experiment seriously. "But I'm tired of being a jerk magnet. It's bad enough that Chase is making a complete fool of himself over me, but now there are a few other boys besides him. It's really making me think less of some of these guys—some of the ones I used to respect."

"Is it possible that it's due to their age?" Chelsea asked as she put up her feet. "My dad's always going on about hormone-driven seventeen-year-old boys. He thinks they should all be locked up until they turn twenty-one."

"Does he honestly think they'll improve by then?"

"I don't know. But maybe their emotional maturity will catch up with their testosterone by then."

Janelle laughed. "So how about Nicholas? I think he's falling in love with Trina."

Chelsea shook her head. "I think he's falling into *like* with Trina."

"Don't be so sure. I've seen him looking at you. It's like he's enchanted."

Now Chelsea felt worried. "But if he knew who I really was . . . he might be enraged."

"Really?"

"Nick has a problem with girls who are too pretty, as he says."

"He's been nice to me."

"Because he's trying."

"So what do you suppose is the root of his problem with hot babes?" Janelle peered over her computer screen.

"He hasn't gone into all the details, but I have a strong feeling he was overly involved with a hot babe."

Janelle's neatly plucked brow creased. "Now that you mention it, I remember that he dated Vanessa Renaldo last year. It was only briefly, but after they broke up, Nicholas seemed different."

"What do you think happened?" Chelsea asked.

"I'm not sure. I can't even remember who broke up with who. Do you think the breakup had to do with sex?"

Chelsea shrugged. Maybe she didn't really want to know about that. But Janelle continued, speculating on Vanessa's reputation and insinuating that Nicholas might've taken advantage of it.

"You know, Janelle . . ." Chelsea went over to the mirror, peering at herself and wondering what it would feel like to remain plain Jane, aka Trina, forever. "You're passing judgments again." Thanks to Trina's dramatic departure from dinner on Friday, combined with Nicholas's efforts, the whole idea of judging others had become a pretty hot topic among the kids at camp.

Janelle sighed. "You're right. I can't believe I just said that. Forget about it, okay?"

Chelsea took off her glasses and rubbed the bridge of her nose. "I have an idea, Janelle."

"Huh?" Janelle looked up from her laptop.

"Let's come clean."

"Come clean?" Janelle pushed her laptop aside. "What do you mean?"

"Let's confess to everyone what we've been doing."

"Are you kidding?" Janelle got to her feet and moved to the mirror, where she stared at her blonde bombshell image with a worried expression. "They'd probably stone us."

"They can't stone us. In fact, they have to forgive us."

Janelle's mouth twisted to one side. "That's true. It's a Christian camp, they'd have to forgive us. But why should we tell them the truth? Everything's been going pretty smoothly. No one suspects a thing."

"But it's not fun anymore," Chelsea reminded her. "You said so." The truth was it had never been much fun for Chelsea.

"That's true. I'm a little sick of Brittany, and these heels are killing me."

"So you agree? It's time to drop the facade?"

"Maybe. But if we do it, we have to do it right."

"Right?"

Janelle nodded. "Yes, we need to make a point, to use what we've done to show these kids how shallow everyone can be." She started clapping her hands. "I know! I know!"

"What?"

"We'll do it like I told my mom. Like it was a skit."

"Huh?"

"We'll go talk to our counselors—to Raymond and Alice. We'll confess the whole thing and ask if we can do something publicly to make a point."

"Do you honestly think they'd agree to something that crazy?"

"They might. Come on. Let's go find them."

They spotted Alice sitting in the sun with some of the other youth group girls. "We can't just walk up and announce what's going on," Chelsea pointed out.

Janelle whipped out her cell phone and called Alice. From a distance they watched as Alice answered. "This is Janelle, but don't let on that you're talking to me," she said quickly. "I'm here at camp, and I have something urgent to talk to you about." She gave Alice their room number and asked her to meet them there, then they hurried back to their room and waited for her to arrive.

"Oh." Alice looked surprised when Janelle answered the door. "I thought this was—"

"It's me, Janelle," she whispered as she grabbed Alice and pulled her into the room and shut the door.

"Wh-what?" Alice looked slightly frightened.

"I'm Janelle." She unpinned the blonde wig and removed it, shaking her brunette hair out. "See?"

Alice's eyes were huge. "Huh?"

"And this is Chelsea." Janelle pointed at Chelsea.

"No way."

Janelle and Chelsea took turns explaining, and before long Alice was laughing so hard that she fell onto a bunk with tears running down her cheeks. Janelle and Chelsea were laughing too. The more they talked about it, the more hilarious it became.

"I can't wait to tell Raymond about this," Alice said finally. "I'm sure he'll want to get in on the action. Keep your phone handy, Janelle—I mean Brittany—and I'll get back to you ASAP."

After Alice left, Janelle decided she wanted one last round of playing Brittany. "You know, in case they decide to pull the plug on us immediately." She chuckled. "I have to jerk that Chase boy around a little more. Just for kicks."

"Have fun," Chelsea called as Janelle left.

A few minutes later, she heard someone knocking on their door. Peeking out the window, she saw it was Nicholas. She checked her wig and makeup and cracked the door open. "Yes?"

"Trina?" he said. "Want to go for a walk on the beach? It's really nice out and the tide's low."

Again she was torn. Of course she wanted to go for a walk with him. But not as Trina. Still, she reminded herself, Trina was really just another version of Chelsea—last year's model, in fact. "Okay. Let me get my shoes."

Before long they were walking on the beach. Fortunately— and unfortunately—Nicholas was not holding her hand. In fact, as it turned out, that had been a onetime thing. She figured it had simply been Nick trying to be brotherly, trying to make Trina feel comfortable and welcome.

"It's been great getting to know you," he told her as they walked along the water's edge. "I hope we can stay in contact."

Chelsea didn't say anything. How was she supposed to respond?

"But I'll understand if you don't want to." He sounded uncomfortable.

"Things aren't always as they seem," she told him meekly.

"What do you mean?" He gave her a sideways glance.

She stopped walking. Turning toward him, she planted her hands on her hips. "For instance, tell me what you see right now."

He smiled. "I see a sweet girl I'd like to know better."

"Why do you want to know me better?"

He looked slightly off balance. "Because you're interesting. You're a good conversationalist. You think more deeply than most girls."

She nodded. She actually liked his response. "And nothing more than that, right?"

His eyes grew wide. "Absolutely. Oh, Trina, you didn't think I was coming on to you, did you?"

She shrugged. "I don't know."

"I'm not. I swear, Trina, I'm not putting a move on you. I just want to be friends."

She sighed. "And that's supposed to make me feel good?"

Now he looked like he'd been caught—stuck between a rock and a hard place.

"Just because I'm plain and dowdy doesn't mean I don't have feelings, Nicholas Prague. Because I do. Whether you know it or not, ugly girls have feelings just the same as pretty ones, and—"

"I never said you were ugly, I just meant—"

"I know what you meant. I know all about boys like you. You think I'm not attractive enough for you to consider for more than just a friend. Right? If you can keep me as a friend, it keeps you in your comfort zone. But how do you think that makes me feel? And what about girls like Olivia? Did you ever stop to think that while you're hanging with Olivia, treating her like your good buddy, she might be nurturing a secret crush on you?"

Nicholas looked stumped.

"Just because a girl is plain or ugly or skinny or fat or has frizzy hair or braces or zits does not mean she doesn't want a guy to like her for more than just a friend. And just because you think you're Mr. Prince Charming does not give you a free pass to wear those plain, ugly, skinny, or fat girls on your arm like a special-needs-friend trophy. Acting like you're such a good guy, such a fine and honorable Christian, that you can lower yourself to be seen with someone like—like me!" She tapped her flattened chest. "Because I have feelings too. Just because I'm plain and ugly does not mean I don't have hopes or dreams for love and romance. So just quit messing with me. And quit taking advantage of girls like me. We are humans too, Nicholas Prague!"

She turned from him and started to run. He called for her to stop, but she didn't. She just kept running like there were wild dogs chasing her, and she didn't stop until she was safely in her room. This time she was determined not to budge from there until it was time to go tomorrow. If Dad and Kate were back, she'd call them and beg to be taken home.

She closed her eyes and felt herself drifting to sleep. If only she could sleep until Sunday.

twenty

C helsea!" Janelle said as she burst into the room. "Where have you been? I've been trying to call you."

Chelsea looked up from the bed, trying to get her bearings, then remembered they were still at fall camp. "I'm right here. What's going on?"

Janelle sat in the chair across from her and explained how Raymond had gotten together with the head counselor, Dirk Erickson, and how they wanted the girls to reveal their true identity at tonight's meeting.

"It's so cool, Chelsea. It turns out that Dirk's message for tonight is all about judging others. So he's really excited about using our experiment for his illustration. We'll be like props." She went on to say that he planned to introduce them at the beginning of the meeting, as if to welcome them. "Then he'll excuse us, and we'll come back here and get back to our normal selves in time for him to reintroduce us and explain what we did. He might even do a little interview with us."

Chelsea sat up. "Hey, that would be kind of cool."

"So you're okay with it?"

Chelsea shrugged. "I'll feel a little silly. But I doubt I could make any worse fool of myself than I already did today."

"What did you do?"

Chelsea told Janelle about the scene on the beach. "I was so pathetic," she said finally, "it probably sounded like I was begging Nicholas to be my boyfriend. And that's not what I meant. I just wanted him to see how he makes us feel."

"That's a good point." Janelle nodded. "Nick is always nice and sweet to me—I mean, when I'm in my own skin, but I see him treating you like . . . well . . ."

"Like I've got cooties."

"Basically. I can't help but feel offended that he's comfortable talking to me like I'm not a threat, like I wouldn't presume to think he might be interested in me for anything besides just a friend."

"Exactly!" Chelsea pointed her finger in the air. "How dense is that?"

"Very." Janelle sat down and put her feet up. "So what did we learn, Chelsea? Or did we learn anything we didn't already know?"

Chelsea thought hard. "I'm not even sure."

"Well, maybe we should think about it. I mean, in case Dirk asks us something like that." Janelle got out her laptop again. "This is going to be a really good paper for psychology."

"I'm going to take a walk," Chelsea told her.

"Dinner is in about an hour," Janelle said.

"I know. See you then." Chelsea went outside, and looking around to be sure no one, especially Nicholas, was around, she headed down one of the many trails, walking until she found a bench and sat down. She'd heard so many things this weekend—including some good teaching about God. But she knew that her focus on her disguise and character had been a distraction, and it had probably hindered her from hearing or learning or absorbing these good things. That made her angry. In some ways, playing plain Trina had been as much of a distraction as when she'd been working hard to turn herself into hot babe Chelsea.

"Dear God," she prayed, "I don't want to be a hot babe, and I don't want to be a plain Jane. I just want to be who you want me to be. Please show me who and what that is. I want to be a person who is more focused on you than myself. Can you teach me to do that?" She prayed awhile longer, and when she finally said, "Amen," she felt a reassuring sense of peace, like maybe she was closer to God than she realized. She felt hopeful, and she believed that he could and would show her who she was. Most of all, she was thankful that she was God's.

It was getting dusky as she came back into the camp. She could tell by the lighted windows in the dining room that dinner was already in progress. She slipped into the back of the already full room, finding a place at one of the quieter tables along the edge. Instead of playing the painfully shy Trina, Chelsea decided to just be herself and act normal. She said hello and introduced herself and made an attempt at conversation. This wasn't exactly easy either since most of the kids at this table seemed to have some real insecurities and self-image issues. But she simply smiled and asked them about themselves, making eye contact and waiting for their responses, and by the time the meal was over, she felt like she'd made some genuine friends.

She saw Nicholas coming her way and was tempted to run

the other direction, but decided not to. She had prayed and asked God to help her find herself, and she wasn't going to go the opposite direction now. "Hi, Nick," she said.

He looked surprised. "Hi, Trina."

"Sorry about my little outburst on the beach." She looked him directly in the eyes and held her head high. "I guess there were a few things I needed to say. But I could've said them a little more gently. I'm sorry."

"No, don't apologize. I've actually given a lot of thought to what you said. It wasn't easy to hear at the time, but the more I considered it, the more I realized you were right."

"Really?" She blinked. "Well, that's cool."

Janelle came up to her. "Hey, darlin', I need to talk to you," she said in her Southern drawl.

Chelsea glanced at Nicholas and smiled. "See you later."

"Yeah." He nodded with a slightly confused expression. "Later."

"We need to do some rehearsing for tonight's gig," Janelle said quietly as she guided Chelsea out of the dining room. "I want to win an Oscar."

"Huh?"

"I'll explain."

Once they were in their room, Janelle told Chelsea the plan. "Dirk texted me, asking if we could beef up our parts a bit, reel the kids in, make it dramatic." She chuckled. "I texted him back saying that we could."

"How?"

"By telling the truth."

"About what?"

Janelle explained her genius plan. "We start out in our roles as Brittany and Trina. We talk about how our reception here felt. How I got lots of attention and you got mostly ignored. Well, except for Nicholas's pity play."

"But we won't mention names, okay?"

"Sure. No problem. In fact, since we're assuming false identities, why not create pseudonyms for others as well? If we need to, we can change the names to protect the innocent."

They started plotting their strategy, and the more they worked, the more fun it became. "It's like a mini play," Chelsea said as they got ready for the eight o'clock meeting.

"How do I look?" Janelle asked her. "My last night as a hot babe."

"You sure you're showing enough cleavage there?" Chelsea teased. "That padded push-up bra should be getting overtime for the work it's doing."

"You should talk. That athletic thing you're wearing is probably getting ready to burst out at the seams."

"Don't remind me. The sooner I'm out of it, the happier I'll be."

They laughed and went out the door, chatting in character as they went to the meeting house. Before long they were being called up from the audience.

"I'd like to introduce a couple of new faces to everyone," Dirk said. "I realize some of you may have met them already, but this is their first camp, and I'd like to hear their reactions. Come on up, Brittany Woodard and Trina Johnson."

The girls went forward. Chelsea reminded herself this was playing a role, like when she played Maggie in drama.

Dirk started with Brittany. "I hear you're from the South, little lady. Tell me what you think of our West Coast kids. The boys treating you all right?"

Janelle giggled nervously. "Well, your boys have been more

than kind," she said into the mike. "They're so friendly and attentive, I can hardly believe it. I walk up to a door, and suddenly three boys are stumbling over each other just to open it for me. I start to sit down to a meal and it's the same thing—boys trying to get me a chair, inviting me to sit right next to them."

Dirk chuckled. "Well, I'm glad the boys are being hospitable. How about the girls?"

"Oh . . . well now, that's a different story."

"How's that?"

"The girls . . ." She frowned. "Besides my good friend Trina here, not a single girl has really spoken to me."

"Probably because we couldn't get past the boys," a girl shouted from the audience.

Janelle nodded. "That might be true. But even when I tried to start up a little chat with some of you girls, y'all just treated me like an outcast, like I was contagious. I'm sorry to say I honestly didn't feel too welcomed by the girls. So naturally, I spent more time with the boys."

"And you found that enjoyable?" Dirk asked.

"I liked it at first." She waved a hand in the air. "But after a while, it got downright overwhelming. All this nonstop male friendliness, the invites to walk the beach . . . oh my! Then I realized some of these boys were under the wrong impression about the kind of girl I am." She covered her mouth with her hand like she was embarrassed to say more.

"Can you explain that better?" Dirk said.

"Oh, you know how it is. Some boys see a girl like me, and they think about one thing and one thing only."

"Really, what's that?"

"I'm embarrassed to say it in front of y'all, but y'all probably know what I mean. You see, some boys take one look at a girl like me, and they automatically assume I have the same thing on my mind as they do. And you know what that is."

The audience broke into giggles and laughter and some comments.

"Meaning the boys want to get romantic with you?" Dirk said in a cornball way. "Steal a kiss or maybe even something more intimate?"

With wide eyes, Janelle nodded. "You mean you used to be a boy too?" More laughter erupted from the audience. "Some boys think that just because I'm blonde, I must be dumb too. And before you know it, innocent hand holding turns into something altogether different." She looked shocked. "And here I thought this was a nice Christian camp."

"Well, you know Christians are human too, Brittany. And boys will be boys. Isn't that right, girls?" Several hoots of yeses and more laughter followed.

Dirk turned to Chelsea. "And how about you, Trina? How has your time here been?"

Chelsea gave a slightly shocked expression. "Not anything like Brittany's, that's for sure." She paused for the laughter.

"The boys weren't chasing after you?" he asked.

"One young man was, uh, friendly," she said carefully. "But I think it was out of pity."

"Pity?" Dirk frowned.

"Because he felt sorry for me. You know, because I'm kind of a wallflower." She sighed. "But I suppose that was better than being ignored."

"Were you ignored?"

She nodded. "Pretty much."

"I'm sorry."

"But I think it's partly my own fault. I think when a person is shy and insecure, it holds people at a distance. In some ways, Brittany and I aren't all that much different."

"How is that?"

"We were both misjudged based on our appearance. Girls kept a distance from Brittany while boys couldn't get close enough—all because of how she looked. At the same time, everyone, except for that one guy who felt sorry for me, avoided me because of the way I look." She looked out at the audience of kids. To her surprise, they seemed to be listening. "Yet no one really knew us—I mean, who Brittany and I truly are on the inside—because they were judging us based on appearances only. They never seemed to get past what they were seeing."

"Do you think that's how Jesus dealt with people?" Dirk asked her in a serious tone. "Judging them based on appearances?"

"I don't know a lot about Jesus—this is still new to me—but I don't think God looks at the outside of people as much as he looks at the inside. But I could be wrong."

Dirk put a hand on her shoulder. "No, you're not wrong. Thanks for sharing, girls." As they left the stage, he began to talk about how Trina was spot-on. "God does look at our hearts, doesn't he? We all know that, and we've heard it time and again. We also know that God wants us to imitate him. Yet over and over, we fall into that trap—we pass judgment on people based on what we can see. As a result, we miss the parts of people that matter."

The girls were outside now. "I wish I could hear the rest of that," Chelsea said as they hurried back to their room.

"It's all taped," Janelle told her. "You can hear it later."

They were barely into their room when they started ripping off their clothes—rather, their costumes—scrambling to help each other with makeup and wigs and hair and all the other details. Fortunately, they'd already laid out some of their regular clothes, which was a challenge considering they had packed mostly for their experiment. Partly because time and wardrobe were limited and partly because Chelsea had no desire to look like a hot babe anymore, she didn't put a lot of effort into her hair and makeup. The result was a more natural look, but compared to plain Trina, it was a great improvement. And thanks to Janelle's eyebrow makeover, she looked a little better than usual too.

For the most part, they were both back to their old selves, and Chelsea felt relieved. She also felt extremely nervous. She wasn't sure if her nerves were the result of her recent Trina act, something that was too close to the truth of her past to be comfortable. Or was she worried about what would come next? It was one thing to stand in front of the crowd and perform an act, but to stand up there and be vulnerable, be herself . . . now that would be a challenge. Even so, Chelsea knew what she had to do—and with God's help, she would do it.

twenty-one

The cat was out of the bag now. Dirk had made his big announcement about the true identities of Brittany and Trina. The crowd's reaction had been mixed—some seemed shocked, others looked curious, a few acted disinterested, and some actually looked angry. Chelsea stood in the shadows, watching as Janelle went forward and explained about the experiment.

"To be honest, I wanted to prove to Chelsea that some girls set themselves up to be a jerk magnet." She paused for some chuckles. "I believed that if a girl dressed a certain way, acted a certain way—like Brittany did—she would attract a certain kind of guy. In other words, a jerk." Janelle laughed, then got sober again. "But I stand by my theory. And I feel I proved it. When I dressed as Brittany the blonde bombshell, I attracted a small crowd of guys who were interested in me for basically one thing, and let's say it wasn't my brilliant mind." More laughter.

"But I learned something else too," Janelle said. "I touched on this before, but I learned that it's really lonely being a jerk magnet. My friend Chelsea, who is something of a jerk magnet in real life, has had great difficulty making friends with girls. Oh, the guys trail her and drool over her and try to date her, but most of the girls—even me at times—try to distance ourselves from her. It's like we're either afraid of her or intimidated by her or just confused. But now I've reached the conclusion that treating a girl like that only makes the problem worse. Because the truth is a jerk magnet needs some good friends." She looked at Chelsea. "Right?"

Chelsea nodded as she walked up to stand by Janelle. "That's absolutely true. It gets lonely when girls treat you like a pariah. And believe it or not, fending off the boys gets a little boring."

"So tell us your story," Dirk said to Chelsea.

She stepped up to the mike and cleared her throat. "Well, my story actually begins several years ago." She confessed how she'd been a total misfit with braces and zits and no friends whatsoever. She couldn't bring herself to mention her complete lack of breasts until age sixteen, but she did admit to being desperately lonely and introverted. "I hated any social situations, and I did all I could to avoid them. I was an extreme wallflower. I worked hard academically, but I worked even harder to stay under the radar—especially of mean girls. I was miserable."

"Tell us what changed you," Dirk said. "You don't seem like the girl you're describing at all now."

"Kate, my stepmother, is very beautiful and stylish. She helped me with a makeover this summer. At first I didn't want it. I thought it was impossible for me to be anything but what I was. But I gave in, and she worked me over. The weird thing is that even when I looked different on the outside, I felt exactly the same on the inside. So Kate gave me some tools and taught me some things to build up my self-confidence. She told me that it wasn't how I looked that mattered as much as how I felt about myself. I don't think I got that right away—to be honest, I was kind of caught up in my new look. But I think I'm starting to get it now."

Chelsea paused. She was surprised to see that everyone seemed to be listening intently to her. "I recently committed my life to God," she said. "And thanks to some things I heard at this camp and some things I've experienced, I've decided that all I want to be is what God wants me to be." She smiled. "I think that's going to take some of the pressure off." She stepped away from the mike.

"Thank you, Janelle and Chelsea," Dirk told them. "Thanks for sharing so transparently with us. What do you think, people? Did anything these girls say resonate with anyone? Put your hands together if you can relate to any part of this." The room erupted in loud applause.

"Now we're going to do something a little different," Dirk said. "We're going to break into small groups and talk about some of the things that Janelle and Chelsea brought up. One of our counselors has put together some group questions, and hopefully we'll have some interesting discussions. We considered separating girls and guys but decided mixed groups might be more revealing. So we ask your co-operation and honesty. If Janelle and Chelsea could stand up here and tell all like they just did, you should be willing to open up some too."

The small groups started out slowly but went on until past midnight. Guys and girls slowly let their guards down and opened up about all kinds of things in regard to self-image problems, confusion about dating, and a lot of other related topics. On Sunday morning, almost everyone agreed that this fall camp was the best one ever, and when it was time to leave and go their separate ways, there was a lot of hugging and even some tears.

"How did your experiment go?" Mrs. Parker asked after they'd loaded their bags in the trunk and were on their way home.

"It was amazing," Janelle told her. Without giving all the details, she filled her in a bit.

Chelsea had to agree, it really was amazing. When she went to school on Monday morning, dressed a little more casually than previously, she felt more natural and relaxed than ever before. She wasn't sure if it was just her imagination or because she was trying harder, but everyone seemed a bit friendlier than usual.

The only person she was unsure about was Nicholas Praguc. He hadn't been in her small group at camp, and she'd been so busy the next day—talking to other girls, sharing more of her story, and answering questions—that she'd never had the chance to speak to him again. The last time she'd actually talked to him, she'd still been playing Trina. Naturally, that alone made her more than a little nervous. Would he feel tricked or betrayed or just plain foolish now?

It was for those reasons that she felt she owed him an apology, and she decided to get it over with during lunch. "Can I talk to you?" she asked when she spotted him coming into the cafeteria with Chase.

"Uh, sure, I guess so." Nicholas looked uneasy, and Chase looked like he was about to make some stupid comment, but then he stopped himself and just smiled.

"Want to go outside?" Chelsea asked.

"Okay." Nicholas pushed the door open for her and followed her out. His expression was somber. Perhaps even bordering on mad, unless it was her imagination.

Saying a silent prayer, Chelsea went over to a quiet corner of the courtyard and sat down on a bench. Without saying anything, Nicholas sat down next to her, but not too close, like he didn't want to accidentally touch her. Or maybe he was trying to distance himself. Not that she blamed him particularly.

"I just want to tell you I'm sorry," she began slowly. "First of all, I'm sorry for deceiving you by playing Trina. I never realized the whole thing would go that far. I'm also sorry for the things I said to you on the beach the other day. Some of them were true, but I know now that some were probably just plain hurtful. I'm sorry for that. But most of all, I'm sorry for kind of tricking you as to my real identity. You were trying to be so sincere, and there were moments when I really wanted to confess what was going on, but that would've ruined the experiment."

"The experiment?" He frowned. "Was that what it really was? Or were you just trying to make a fool out of me?"

Chelsea thought about that. "To be perfectly honest . . . it might've been a bit of both. Not that I specifically wanted to embarrass you. But I did want to show you that you were being totally unfair to me. When I heard you and the others talking about me at dinner that night—I mean, the way they were talking about Chelsea while I was pretending to be Trina—well, that hurt. It hurt a lot. Then when you said those things to me, thinking I was Trina but talking about Chelsea like you did—that hurt too. It's like you managed to hurt both Chelsea and Trina simultaneously—if that makes any sense. I suppose I thought that gave me the right to take the charade to the next level. But anyway, I'm sorry if I hurt you, Nicholas. I would've apologized to you at camp, but I never really saw you again." She stood now. "I'm truly sorry, and I hope you'll forgive me someday."

"So are you just going to walk away now?" He stood too and looked at her with a slightly exasperated expression.

"I think I've said all I need to say." She slipped her hands into her jacket pockets.

"Well, I'd like to say something too." He tipped his head to the bench. "Care to sit down again?"

She shrugged. "Okay."

"Well, as usual, you beat me to the punch, Chelsea. I wanted to apologize to you too. I tried to find you at camp yesterday, but you were always surrounded by your adoring fans and—"

"My adoring fans?" She narrowed her eyes. Was this an apology or another lecture?

"Sorry." He looked slightly embarrassed. "I mean your friends. But you have to admit they were kind of like a fan club. After all, you and Janelle were the camp celebrities— whether you were playing Brittany and Trina or just being yourselves, you had everyone going. And it's not like I blame any of your followers because, seriously, you girls did a great job on Saturday night. Kudos to you."

"Thanks . . . I guess."

"So anyway, I wanted to apologize to you, Chelsea. I have to admit that you hit the nail on the head with me more than once. First on Friday night when you defended girls like Chelsea, and then on Saturday when you went to bat for girls like Trina." He shook his head. "Mostly I feel like an ignorant buffoon around you."

She blinked. "Seriously? An ignorant buffoon?"

He smiled. "It's like I've been trying so hard to do the right thing—you know, like, I've been overthinking everything—and as a result, I've been a total ignoramus."

She couldn't help but laugh now.

"It's humbling to sit here and admit all this, but I said pretty much the same thing in my small group—and several of the people there agreed wholeheartedly with me. I'm sure you do too."

"Oh, Nicholas." She shook her head. "Your heart's in the right place. But I think you could be right, you might be overthinking things." She sighed. "The truth is I can relate to that. I've done a lot of overthinking myself. It's always been a challenge for me to figure out where I fit in. I mean, you heard what I said on Saturday night. That was the truth—but I was even more of an outcast than I admitted to. And trying to figure things out now, plus being a new Christian as well . . . it's not exactly a walk in the park, if you know what I mean."

He nodded. "I do know what you mean."

She stuck out her hand. "So do you think we can be friends?"

His face broke into a gorgeous grin as he grasped her hand and firmly shook it. "Nothing would make me happier, Chelsea. Thanks for giving me a second chance."

"Isn't that what life is all about? Second chances?" She couldn't help but notice he was still holding her hand—not that she minded, although it did make her heart race a bit.

"That's right. We serve the God of second, third, fourth, and thousandth chances, so I guess we should imitate him, right?"

"Right." Chelsea didn't know what to do—he was still holding her hand! "Anyway, I'm glad we can be friends, Nicholas. I'd really like to get to know you better. And I'd like you to know the real me." She giggled nervously. "To be honest, it's partly Chelsea and partly Trina—I think I'm still figuring it out myself."

He smiled. "I like that combination." He seemed to realize he was still holding her hand. "Sorry." He slowly released her fingers, looking slightly embarrassed. "Want to go get some lunch now?"

She nodded. As they walked to the cafeteria together, she felt a rush of emotions—hope and happiness and so many other interesting things. But mostly, and most incredibly, she felt almost completely comfortable in her own skin. Besides that, and perhaps for the first time, she felt thankful—truly thankful—that God had made her exactly as he did.

Melody Carlson is the award-winning author of over two hundred books for adults, teens, and children. She is the author of many novels for teens, including *Just Another Girl* and *Anything but Normal*, as well as several series for teens, including Diary of a Teenage Girl, TrueColors, Notes from a Spinning Planet, the Carter House Girls, and Words from the Rock. She has won a Gold Medallion Award and a Romance Writers of America Rita Award, and she was nominated for a *Romantic Times* Career Achievement Award. She lives with her husband in Sisters, Oregon. Visit her website at www.melodycarlson.com.

Come Meet Melody at
www.MelodyCarlson.com

··

- Enter a contest for a signed book
- Read her monthly newsletter
- Find a special page for book clubs
- And much more

Become a fan on Facebook

 Melody Carlson Books

What do you do when your life's not all it's cracked up to be?
Get a new one.

Worlds collide when a Manhattan socialite and a simple Amish girl meet and decide to switch places.

Revell
a division of Baker Publishing Group
www.RevellBooks.com

Available wherever books are sold.

New School = New Chance for That First Kiss

Just when it seems Elise is on top of the world, everything comes crashing down. Could one bad choice derail her future?

Revell
a division of Baker Publishing Group
www.RevellBooks.com

Available wherever books are sold.

Girls know all about keeping secrets, but Sophie's is a really big one.

Visit Melody Carlson at www.melodycarlson.com.

 Revell
a division of Baker Publishing Group
www.RevellBooks.com

Available wherever books are sold.

Aster Flynn Wants a Life of Her Own . . .

But will her family get in her way?

Revell
a division of Baker Publishing Group
www.RevellBooks.com

Available wherever books are sold.

Be the First to Hear about Other New Books from Revell!

Sign up for announcements about new and upcoming titles at

www.revellbooks.com/signup

Follow us on **twitter**
RevellBooks

Join us on **facebook**.
Revell

Don't miss out on our great reads!

Revell
a division of Baker Publishing Group
www.RevellBooks.com